Death on the Hour

by Richard Lockridge

D0064974

J. B. Lippincott Company
New York and Philadelphia

U.S. Library of Congress Cataloging in Publication Data

Lockridge, Richard, birth date
    Death on the hour.

    I. Title.
PZ3.L81144Dee   [PS3523.O245]   813'.5'2   74–2173
ISBN–0–397–00989–5

For Hildy

1

HE KNOCKED AT THE DOOR between their offices. After almost two years it was a courtesy which still a little surprised her. Before she had come to IBC she had usually been buzzed for. Or the head of the pool had said, sometimes sharply, "Miss Osborne! Mr. Jones's office." Or Mr. Smith's. Or even Mr. Lawrence's. Of course, she was an "assistant" now, no longer a secretary. Not even a private one.

She said, "Yes, Mr. Carter," and her voice rose a little on the words. Her voice was not quite her office voice. The slip bothered her somewhat. But there was nobody except Clayton Carter to hear any difference in her voice, and he must have grown used to her non-office voice. He listened to voices; voices were important to him—voices and the words they framed.

He opened the door and she looked across the room at him—looked at the face millions of men and women looked at five nights a week at seven o'clock Eastern (six o'clock Central) Time. And looked, too, when rockets were being shot at the moon and words being rasped over PA systems by politicians. (And, for the most part, not being much listened to by other politicians in convention assembled.)

He looked at her and smiled. There were not millions familiar with that smile on Clayton Carter's face. Under the lights, in front of the cameras, there had not been, for a good many years, much to smile about—not, at any rate, for Clayton Carter, a director and head of the news department of the Independent Broadcasting Company, youngest and still, by a slowly diminishing margin, smallest, of the networks. To be sure, one of its Washington correspondents who reported on "The News Tonight" had been investigated by the FBI, a distinction IBC shared with CBS. But CBS was bigger. There could be no doubt of that. It owned its five television stations; had many times as many affiliates. And as for radio outlets, there was no real comparison. But the FBI intrusion had been welcome to IBC executives, most of all to Clayton Carter. No network likes to be ignored.

Standing in the doorway, smiling across the small room toward his assistant, Carter had an almost oblong face, with a square, somewhat stubby jaw at the bottom of it. He had a wide and noticeably flexible mouth. His eyes were blue and his short hair blond. He looked to be in his early forties, which was what he was.

He said, "Quitting time, Miss Osborne," and each syllable of the words was precise, immaculate.

She looked at the watch on her wrist. She said, "Already?" He nodded, and she stood up behind her desk. She stood rather tall and slimly rounded. Her hair was long and as blond as Carter's, her eyes a darker blue.

8

Carter's smile widened and he nodded again, not this time to affirm that the time was twelve-fifteen of a Saturday afternoon, late in the month of July.

"We'll stop for lunch on the way," Carter said. "You've got your gear?"

She said, "Yes, Mr. Carter," in very much her office voice, and moved from behind her desk to the office's small closet. Watching her move, Clayton Carter nodded his head again.

She took a small suitcase, with a tennis racket strapped to it, out of the closet. She said, "You're sure Dr. Streeter expects me to—tag along?"

"Entirely sure," Carter said. " 'Bring a partner for mixed doubles if it isn't raining. This Miss Osborne of yours, if she plays.' It isn't raining. Paul's a bunny and Agnes isn't much better. But they're rather proud of their new court. It could be cooler up there."

"It could be cooler almost any place," Janet Osborne said. "Except possibly hell itself."

She started toward the door, carrying her small suitcase with the covered tennis racket strapped to it. Clayton Carter took the case from her and followed her through the door into his larger corner office and from it into the corridor of the nineteenth floor. It was only moderately cool in the corridor. It was not cool at all in the elevator, in spite of an anxious little fan. On the Madison Avenue sidewalk, it was New York City in a late July heat wave. But they stood on the sidewalk for only a minute or two before the car came up from the basement garage. The car jockey had remembered to turn on the air conditioning and got a dollar for his memory.

It grew cooler in the car as Carter turned left in Fifty-seventh Street toward the West Side Highway. It was cool, too, in the restaurant off the Saw Mill River

Parkway. Their table overlooked the Saw Mill River, a trickle in late July. The waiter brought them cocktail glasses and what looked like very miniature milk bottles with water in them. Clay took an olive out of his glass and Janet took a lemon twist out of hers, and they poured from the little bottles into the glasses. When the glasses were full, there was still martini in the little bottles.

"Trick of the trade," Clay said. "You're supposed to think you're getting a dividend."

The drinks were cold. "Tell me about Dr. and Mrs. Streeter," Janet said, after they had clicked their glasses together. "What's he a doctor of, Clay?"

"A Ph.D. sort of doctor," Clay Carter told her. "In social sciences—something like that. It's turned out to be radio and television in Paul's case. On the West Coast until a few years ago. He came east a while back. Recently, he's been a professor of public communications at Dyckman University. Whatever that means. One of those the Administration calls effete intellectuals? The Eastern establishment. Expert witness before a Senate committee a year ago. Committee looking into conglomerates buying up the news media. Not exactly a pet of the Administration, Paul isn't."

He finished his drink. He looked at Janet Osborne's only half-emptied glass. She smiled across the table and shook her head.

"He sounds like a good guy," she said. "The right enemies."

"Ours, anyway," Carter said. He motioned to a waiter, who brought menus—very large menus. Carter indicated his glass. Janet put a hand over hers and shook her head. The waiter said, "Sir. Madam," and went away.

"I've known Paul Streeter since he came east," Clay Carter said. "Talked to one of his classes a while back. We more or less hit it off. More rather than less, actually. Thank you." The last was to the waiter for another glass, olive and mini-bottle.

Janet sipped from her half-emptied glass and looked at the menu. She said, "Do you suppose they're really bay scallops? Or sea scallops cut up?" She looked across at him. "We have suspicious minds, haven't we?" she said.

"Occupational hazard," he told her. "Commercial allergy. But I think I'll chance the scallops."

They both chanced the scallops. They appeared to be from a bay.

She looked out the window at the Saw Mill River. Two small boys were fishing in it. She said it looked too shallow for a fish.

"Well," Clay said, "they're very small boys."

In her year as Clayton Carter's secretary, her ten months as his assistant, Janet had grown accustomed to the quirkiness of his mind. It was quite in order that only very small boys should angle for shallow fish. She nodded and smiled in appreciation of Clay's logic. She finished her scallops.

"I've a feeling I ought to know about Dr. Streeter," she said. "Ought to have heard of him. More than that his name is vaguely familiar. And that his tennis isn't very good."

"No backhand," Carter said. "There was a good deal in the New York *Chronicle* about his testimony at the Senate hearing. He took a dim view of conglomerates buying up news media. So does the *Chronicle*. The *Chronicle* more or less nominated him for the next Federal Communications Commission vacancy.

When old Hopkins bows out. Very grave about it, the *Chronicle* was. Also very tongue-in-cheek, of course."

"Why tongue-in-cheek?"

"Paul Streeter? With this Administration?" There was derision in Carter's flexible voice. "Where do you keep yourself, girl?"

"All right," Janet said. "Tongue-in-cheek, Clay? You want to send me back to the typists' pool?"

"I'll bear it in mind," Carter said, with gravity. "Watch your step, Miss Osborne. Paul's in his late forties, with just that becoming touch of gray at the temples. And it would be a friendly gesture not to play too much to his backhand. In a tactful sort of way. He's a nice guy. Also a perceptive guy."

"I'm not really an idiot, Clay."

His responding smile was slow. It held until her lips answered it. Then he said, "No, Jan. Not really. Do we want dessert? Or just coffee? We've time to kill. If I don't get lost, that is. Three-thirtyish, Agnes said."

"Just coffee for me," Janet said. "We can linger over it, the way people are supposed to. You've not been to the Streeters' before?"

"Not to their new house. They've only been in it a couple of months. Housewarming party a couple of weeks ago. On a Friday, which let me out, of course. This is by way of being a rain check."

"Another party?"

"One other couple, Agnes said. A man named Simmons, it sounded like. And girl friend, I gathered. Like Carter and—"

"And assistant," Janet said.

He shrugged. The waiter brought the menus back, and Carter waved them off and said, "Just coffee."

They did linger over coffee. It was a quarter of three when they were back in the car, which had got hot standing in the sun. Carter thumbed the windows down, and warm air stirred in the car. He turned the air conditioner on and took a folded sheet of paper from his jacket pocket and unfolded it on the seat beside him. He said, "How are you at reading maps?"

She said, "Terrible," and picked the map up. She said, "But it looks clear enough. First left after Mt. Kisco Avenue."

They rolled onto the Parkway and on it north and east. They turned left—except it was a right and an underpass—off the Saw Mill beyond Mt. Kisco Avenue and, after two red lights, were out of the town's traffic.

"Left on Pinetree Lane," Janet said, raising her eyes from the map. "It ought to be along here some—there it is, Clay. Behind that lilac bush." Carter turned the car left beyond the lilac bush.

"Four and three-tenths miles," Janet said. "They're on the right. The mailbox is on the left and their name's on it. It's pretty here. Is this still Westchester?"

"Pretty," Clay agreed, his eyes on the rather narrow, considerably winding, blacktop road. "Still Westchester." He sounded his horn as they went into a blind curve.

"If both cars do that," Janet said, "nobody hears anybody." Clay made an agreeing "Mmmm."

A sign said "Hidden Driveway." They crept around a curve. "Streeter" was lettered on a big mailbox. It wasn't, Janet noted with some relief, "*The* Streeters." They turned beyond a big maple tree on a graveled drive which rose gently to a gray house. It was low for a two-story house and stretched wide. To the right of the house, as they approached it, was a tennis court. There was nobody on the court. Clay swung the car to the left on a graveled turnaround and cut the engine. A trim woman dressed for tennis came out of the house toward the car, and Clay reached over and rolled the window down on Janet's side.

The woman in the white tennis dress said, "Hi." There was a pleased ring in the sound.

Clayton Carter said, "Hi, Agnes." Agnes smiled. "This is Janet Osborne," Carter said. "Agnes Streeter, Jan."

Janet said, "Mrs. Streeter," and took the tanned, slim—and unexpectedly hard—hand held out to her. She said, "Such a beautiful place, Mrs. Streeter."

"We like it," Agnes Streeter said. "You brought your things?"

"As ordered," Clay said. Janet released the latch on her side and Agnes Streeter pulled the door open. Janet stood, several inches taller than Agnes. They started toward the house, and a man in tennis shorts and shirt came out of it.

He was tall and lean and, as Clay had promised, the gray which was creeping into his brown hair at the temples was "becoming." He came down one step from flagstones to gravel and said, "Give you a hand, Clay?"

Carter was coming around the car with a light suitcase in either hand, a racket strapped to each suitcase. He slumped both shoulders to indicate that he was carrying just bearable weight. He said, "I can just about make it, Paul. Jan, this is Paul Streeter I've been telling you about."

"Miss Osborne," Streeter said. "He's been telling us about you, too."

There are conventional remarks to which there is no acceptable response. Janet smiled toward Agnes Streeter, who led the way into the house—into a moderately large room with a staircase rising out of it. It was cool in the room.

"We can have a drink," Agnes said. "Or we can

get in a set before Bernie and Miss Curran get here. Or we can just go out and sit by the pool, if you'd rather."

"Tennis," Paul Streeter said, from just behind them. "Unless they'd rather not, of course." He added, "While the light's good."

"Of course," Janet said, for both of them.

She followed Agnes Streeter up the stairs, carrying her case with the racket strapped to it and, briefly, down a corridor.

"In here, dear," Agnes said. She opened a door, and Janet went into a small bedroom. "Bathroom," Agnes said, needlessly, and gestured toward the bathroom's open door. "Just call if you need anything."

Agnes went out and closed the door behind her.

There was a single large window in the small room. As she unstrapped her racket from the case, Janet glanced out. The tennis court—red, "all weather" surface, tape-lined—was below her. Paul Streeter was sitting on a director's chair on the far side of the court, in partial shade but with long legs stretched out into the sun. His cased racket was on the grass beside the chair. Looking down at him, Janet had a momentary feeling of familiarity. The feeling was only a flicker— the vaguest of flickers, vaguely from the past. It died away as she changed. She had forgotten it as she carried her racket down the stairs and out into the sun.

A car was coming up the drive, and as she walked around the corner of the house toward the court, Streeter was coming toward her. And again there was a momentary feeling of recognition. But it was as insubstantial and fleeting as before.

"Good," Streeter said. "We'll be with you in a couple of minutes."

He went on toward the car, which had pulled

up beside Carter's. Presumably, Janet thought, Bernie Somebody and Miss Somebody Curran. She went on to the court and walked across it. A little soft under-foot, as composition courts sometimes are. Rather slow bounces, probably, which would mean a good deal of running. But the backstops were covered with dark green canvas.

A good deal of money had gone into the court, she thought absently. Into the whole place, come to that. University professors were obviously more prosperous than she had supposed them to be.

There were several director's chairs on the far side of the court and two chaises. She sat on one of the chairs and stretched long brown legs out into the after-noon sun. She waited only a few minutes before Clay Carter, wearing tennis shorts and shirt, with a white sweater draped on his right shoulder, joined her. He had his racket in his right hand and the "gimmick" in the other.

The gimmick was a miniature radio–television set, with a tiny screen. It could be played on batteries or could be plugged in to any 110-volt socket. Where Clayton Carter went the gimmick went. Now he put it down on the grass beside the chair next to Janet's and sat on the chair and stretched his legs into the sunshine.

"Got quite a place, haven't they?" he said. "Hell of a long way up from his old—"

He broke off. The Streeters were coming around the corner of the house. A man and a girl were walking with them. The man was taller than Streeter by some inches. He had the reddest hair Janet Osborne had ever seen. With the sun on it, it looked as if the top of his head were on fire. He was as lean as Paul Streeter, and the leanness was accentuated by his height. The girl wore a sleeveless yellow dress. She had short dark-brown hair and was slim under the yellow dress.

Carter stood up as the four walked toward them. They momentarily disappeared behind the green backstop. The redheaded man and the girl weren't shod to walk across the court. The four came down beside the court, and then Janet, too, stood up. Everybody smiled the expectant smiles of those about to be introduced.

The slim young woman was Nora Curran and, Janet guessed, in her middle twenties. (And Clay didn't have so evidently to devote the full attention of his eyes to her, although Janet could, with only slight effort, see his point.) The man was Bernard Simmons.

"Watch out for him, he embodies the law," Streeter said, which, to Janet, was obscure without being funny.

The redheaded man had a wide, sharable smile. Everybody repeated the names of those newly met.

"Mabel will show you where to change," Agnes Streeter said. "And get you something long and cold. Then come back out and sit in the shade and watch us miss tennis balls."

Streeter was keying open a can of balls as Simmons and Nora Curran walked behind the backstop toward the house.

"Ag and I usually play together, if that's all right?" It was all right. "Spin for serve?" That was all right, too. Clay Carter spun his racket. Streeter called "Rough" and won. A little unexpectedly, he walked ahead of his wife toward the south court, where he would serve with the sun at his back. Wants it both ways, Janet thought.

They rallied idly for a few minutes. Agnes chopped her forehand; her husband's drive had a little top spin. Streeter said "O.K.?" and Clay said "Any time." Janet stood near the baseline to receive. Of course, Streeter might be a man who babied women in mixed doubles.

He was not. He served deep to her forehand. The service was not heavy and the bounce, if unexpectedly low, was honest. Janet drove down the line, hard, and the ball landed deep in the alley. Streeter lunged for it and landed and got his racket on the ball. It went up into the air toward Clay, who seemed to Janet to have set himself for the obvious smash. If he had, he changed his mind. He hit moderately past Agnes, and Streeter got to it. But his drive, aimed between them, was deep by several inches.

I forgot I wasn't to play to his backhand, Janet thought, moving up to the service line. But it's choice of service *or* court.

Streeter double-faulted to Clay. Love–30. His first service to Janet was again to her forehand but not so deep. Streeter started toward the alley but reversed in time to be waiting for Janet's cross-court past Agnes. His forehand drive zoomed toward Janet, but Clay poached, intercepting, and his volley behind Agnes, who had crossed, ended the point. Dr. Streeter anticipates well, Janet thought. They've played a good deal together. Streeter served. He was ready for Clay's backhand return of service, down the line and in the alley. He put up a lob, but it was short and Janet put it away with an overhead.

If the male in mixed doubles does not hold service, tennis becomes merely outdoor exercise. Janet thought that as they changed courts. Clay's first service showed her that he thought that too. It was not his flat serve. It was gentle, almost a floater, with only a little twist. Agnes drove hard between them—and drove, Janet thought, several inches over the base line. But Clay said "Too good!" on a note of admiration.

All right, we baby them, Janet thought. It's still fun to run and hit tennis balls.

The score was 4–1—Janet had dropped her first service, partly because of her efforts to keep the ball on Paul Streeter's forehand—when Bernard Simmons and the slim brown-haired girl, both dressed for tennis, came out to sit on shaded chairs. Neither of them carried glasses containing anything long and cold.

The set ended 6–2. (Clay double-faulted a service away, trying out a twist Janet had never known him to use before.)

"Now you four," Agnes said, as they waited off court. "And Paul and I'll get things set up." She looked at her husband, and Paul Streeter said, "Sure. Before the light gets too bad."

They wouldn't have to baby the stringy red-haired man and Nora Curran. Janet knew that after they had rallied briefly. Clay won the toss and elected to serve—to serve into the sun. He held service, but only after they had gone three times to deuce. After they had changed courts, Simmons held service more easily. He followed his service in; his partner dropped back and was very steady from deep court.

They played to 6–all, and by then the sun was blinding in the north court.

"Does anybody want to play to, maybe, twenty-eighteen?" Simmons asked.

Nobody did. And nobody suggested sudden death. They walked toward the house.

Inside, the men went down a corridor, and Janet and Nora Curran climbed the stairs.

"I'm in here," Janet said at the door to the room Agnes had assigned her. "Is Mr. Simmons a judge or something?"

"A judge or—?" Nora said. "Oh, that crack of Paul's. No, he's an assistant district attorney."

2

IT WAS ALMOST SIX when they gathered on the shaded terrace behind the house and beside the swimming pool. Sunlight slanted across the pool, not "Olympic"-size but large enough. When Janet reached the terrace, and stretched on a chaise with a small glass-topped table beside it, the Streeters were already there, both with drinks beside them. Paul Streeter, in white polo shirt and dark green slacks, was on his feet at once.

"We didn't wait," he said. "What'll it be?" Then, speaking beyond her, "And what's yours, my friend?"

Clay Carter put his gimmick down on the flagstones beside a chair, near Janet's chaise. For a moment he sat, saying nothing, looking across the pool at rolling green hills with sunlight on them. He turned and looked at Janet. He raised his eyebrows and, just perceptibly, she nodded her head. He said, "Whew!" softly and looked up at Paul Streeter, who was smiling down at him.

"Nice hills," Clay said. "*Very* nice hills. Gin and tonic?"

"We like them," Streeter said. "Coming up. Miss Osborne?"

She said that gin and tonic would be fine, and Streeter walked to the end of the terrace and to a table with bottle on it, and glasses and a tall, silvery ice bucket.

"Did you find everything you needed, dear?" Agnes said.

"Everything."

"Bernie and Miss Curran had a swim before they changed," Agnes said. "I should have asked if you wanted to—both of you. I'm so sorry."

She was assured there was nothing to be sorry about.

"I didn't even say you should bring swim things," Agnes said. "I'm terrible. I suppose—well, that I'm not quite used to things yet."

She was told she was not terrible. Paul Streeter brought drinks in tall glasses. There were beads of cold on the glasses. He put the glasses down on the tables.

"I'll tell Mabel about the—" Agnes said, and stopped because a young woman, trim in a white uniform, was coming from the house with a large tray in her hands. A long arm was holding the door open for her. The very-red-haired man came out after her.

"Thank you, Mabel," Agnes Streeter said. "Just put it down over there. We'll help ourselves."

Mabel put the tray down on a glass-topped table beside the bar table. She said, "Anything else, ma'am? The hot ones are in."

"When they're ready, dear." (Everybody was

"dear" to Agnes Streeter, Janet thought. And it's really a beautiful place.)

Bernard Simmons joined Streeter at the bar. He doesn't look like an assistant district attorney, Janet thought. His hair's too red.

He was wearing a polo shirt, as were the other two men. His was yellow—about, as Janet remembered, the same shade of yellow as Miss Curran's dress—*Nora* Curran, that was it.

"Nora'll be along any minute," Simmons said. "We couldn't pass up the pool. Not much chance in the city." He sat on a director's chair near Clayton Carter's and put his glass down on the table beside it. He looked down at the gimmick between them and then at Carter. He raised red eyebrows. He has a very friendly face, Janet thought. I'd have thought district attorneys would have severe faces. Even assistant district attorneys.

"The world's smallest TV set," Clay said, in response to the eyebrows. "Also AM and FM radio. And it's also a tape recorder. By way of being—oh, call it my tool kit, Counselor."

"What will the Japs think up next, do you suppose?" Simmons said.

"German, actually," Carter told him.

"Same adverse balance of trade," Bernard Simmons said. "As you point out from time to time."

Anonymity is impossible to television newscasters. It is not, of course, greatly desired. But it was evident, also, that Clay Carter knew who and what Bernard Simmons was. At the restaurant he had been uncertain about the name. Identified by Paul Streeter? Or identified when seen? I'm almost sure I've seen Dr. Streeter somewhere before, Janet thought. It keeps on being an annoying tickle in my mind.

"You look thoughtful," Paul Streeter said. He was sitting across the terrace, his back to pool and green hills. "Drink all right?"

"Just admiring the view, Doctor," she said. "It's a beautiful place. A serene sort of place. And the drink's fine."

Streeter turned in his chair and looked at the distant hills, as if to verify that they were beautiful with the late afternoon sunlight on them. He turned back and nodded his head slightly.

" 'Paul,' not 'Doctor,' if you'd just as soon," he said. "Yes, we like it. Bought it only recently. Clay may have told you that. I had an ancient aunt who died. Nice old girl, Aunt Emily was. Rich old girl too. So, the kind of place we'd never expected to have. House, court and pool. We were damn lucky to find it. Excuse me. Think I see an empty glass."

She said, "Of course." She added "Paul" to it.

The empty glass was Paul's wife's. He took it to the bar. He tossed fragments of ice from the glass onto clipped grass at the end of the terrace and made another gin and tonic. Mabel brought out a tray with the "hot ones" on it. They were of toasted cheese and, Janet thought, crab meat on little squares of toast. They were very good.

"You work with Mr. Carter," Nora Curran said, from her chaise next to Janet's. "I gathered that from Agnes."

"They call me an assistant to the producer. Mostly I go over what the news writers turn in. Sort them out and—oh, put queries on them for him. Something for him to work on. Rewrite. Put in a different order if he wants to. He usually does."

Nora nodded her head as she listened.

"A little like what I do," Nora Curran said. "At

a different tempo, of course. Yours must be—oh, all crammed together."

"Between six and air time things do get a little rushed. And when he's on the air sometimes there are bulletins to feed him. There's often pressure, of course."

"He never shows it," Nora said. "Not on the air, I mean. He always seems so assured. No, that's not quite right. 'Certain' is probably more what I mean. On top of things. He's very good, I think. I watch him almost every night. He's—oh, on my side, I suppose. Or I'm on his."

"Not everybody is," Janet said. "Take the FBI, for example. They've been trying to find out who one of our Washington boys sleeps with. Rather funny, because he's only been married about a year, and I'd suppose—" She let it trail off with that, because she thought Nora Curran had stopped listening. At any rate, Nora was looking at the green hills.

"I don't have to take the FBI," Nora said, a little as if she were speaking to herself. "Not yet, anyway." She lifted slender shoulders a little under the yellow dress. She turned back to Janet.

"I'm an editor at Materson and Brothers," Nora said. "They're book publishers. And I'm just an assistant editor, actually. Did you ever hear of something called the Bartwell Industries, Miss Osborne?"

"Actually, I used to work there," Janet said. "Main office. New York office, anyway. Stenographic pool. Why, Nora?"

"There's a rumor they're about to buy out Materson," Nora Curran said. "It's—well, some of us are worried. It's an old firm, Materson is. A hundred years old. Traditions. That sort of thing. There actually is a Materson on the board of directors. And to be—swallowed up."

"Conglomerates have big mouths," Janet said. "Oil companies. Wheat farms. Railroads and breweries and hotel chains and companies that make paper clips. And newspapers and magazines. At least Bartwell does. There aren't really any Bartwells around, as far as I know. There was one once, I think. He made sewer pipe, somebody told me when I was working there. Now one of the things they do is build ships for the Navy. With some outsize overruns. We did a special on that a while back. Clay's—that is, Mr. Carter's idea. Taking over Materson and Brothers?"

"It's not final yet, far's I know," Nora Curran said. "Or perhaps it is, and just hasn't seeped down to me. Nothing to be surprised about, I suppose. Publishing has been cannibalistic the last few years. Still, to be gobbled up by something—oh, impersonal, like an overgrown computer—something like Bartwell—"

"It is like a computer," Janet said. "One reason I was glad to get out. To go to IBC. It's—well, it's itself, if you know what I mean."

Nora Curran knew what she meant.

"So was Materson," Nora said. "Itself, and a tough self. A year ago it told the FBI to go fly a kite."

Janet shook her head.

"It was in the papers," Nora said. "In the *Chronicle* anyway. I thought IBC covered it."

"I was new there a year ago," Janet said. "Not much into things. And I guess I miss things in the *Chronicle*. Told the FBI to go fly a kite? Did it?"

"Sort of, I guess. You see—"

What Janet was to see was that a former FBI agent had submitted a book to Materson & Brothers—a book about the FBI. A not very laudatory book. "A good book, we thought. Perhaps even an important book." The book was in proof when a special agent of the FBI showed up. The FBI wanted to see proofs before publication. It feared that "national security might be jeopardized."

"The way he put it, according to Mr. Baker. Theodore Baker. He's head of trade books."

The FBI man had, at first, said that the Bureau only wanted to check for accuracy. The involvement of the national security came in later. And Theodore Baker had said, "Not without a court order." The agent had gone to the president of Materson & Brothers and been told the same thing.

"They didn't try to get a court order," Nora said. "They didn't get to see the proofs. We published the book. It got a few good reviews—sold pretty well. Not as well as we'd hoped. And now Bartwell is maybe taking us over. Probably no connection, I suppose."

For a moment, Janet looked at the distant green hills. Then she said, "There was quite a stink about our Bartwell special on the overruns. Some Administration spokesman said it was 'liberal plugola.' And—"

"You two seem pretty serious about something," Paul Streeter said, standing in front of them. "And with empty glasses." Janet could only guess how long Streeter had been standing in front of them, waiting for them to finish, waiting to offer drinks.

"No," Nora Curran said. "Just—basking. Could I have a martini this time, Dr. Streeter?"

"Paul."

"Paul," Nora said.

"Martini it is," Streeter said. "Janet?"

"If you're going to make them," Janet said. "Up?"

"No other civilized way," Streeter said, and picked up their empty glasses. "Two martinis up." He carried the glasses to the bar. He stirred in a mixer, and the rattling ice was a pleasant sound on the quiet terrace;

the now almost cool terrace. Agnes passed canapés. Janet was conscious of slight movement in the chair on her right. Clayton Carter was looking at the watch on his wrist. She looked at hers. It lacked a few minutes of seven.

"I hope nobody minds," Carter said. "I'll keep it low." He reached down to the gimmick.

"Outlet down there," Streeter said, coming from the bar with a stemmed glass in either hand. He moved the glass in his right hand in a pointing gesture.

"Do all right on batteries," Carter said. "Anyway I think it will."

He lifted the little TV set to the table beside him, putting his glass on the flagstones to make room for it. He turned a knob, and the set groaned softly for a moment or two. Then its tiny screen lighted up. After another moment a woman's head and shoulder appeared on the screen. They were miniature. There was a tiny sound. "And take Geritol every day," the set whispered.

Carter turned a knob. "And you should too," the set told him, in a slightly enhanced whisper.

The screen was blank for a moment. Then there was the sound of a siren and a picture of a man being thrown through a window, glass shattering around him. Almost instantly the screen showed a man firing a machine gun at a group of men, several of whom clutched at themselves as they fell. "Watch *The Barbarians*, a world premiere motion picture at nine-thirty Central Time, right here on IBC." For a moment, the little screen was merely a lighted oblong. Then men and women moved on it, among desks. Superimposed were the words, "The IBC News Tonight" and, fading in, "With Ronald Latham."

Ronald Latham wore a broadly striped shirt and long sideburns, and he was in black and white. The tiny set stopped short of color. Latham shuffled papers. He pulled up jacket sleeves to reveal shirt cuffs. He said, "Good evening. This is the news tonight. In the Middle East—" As he said the words, a picture of Golda Meir appeared behind him.

Things were no better than usual in the Middle East, but there was a correspondent to tell about them via satellite. Things were not noticeably better anywhere or, for that matter, perceptibly different. They were not noticeably different in Washington. Administration officials foresaw a continued upward surge in the economy and urged restraint by labor in its demands —oh, and restraint, too, by the business community. It would also, of course, be necessary for the Congress to behave responsibly.

"And now," said Ronald Latham, turning full-face to the camera (he had been looking toward his right, rather obviously at a monitor), "for the reaction of Congressional leaders to the latest Administration statements, we go to Milton Oberloff on Capitol Hill."

Milton Oberloff wore a broadly checked sports jacket, and the Capitol of the United States was behind him.

Congressional reaction was mixed. The minority leader of the Senate was certain that the Congress would stand united behind the President of the United States; his inflection seemed to bestow sainthood. He also expected an early adjournment if petty objections to special appropriations for the Department of Defense, so necessary to keep this nation strong, could be dropped in the interest of harmony.

The majority leader of the Senate said, "Yah," in somewhat more numerous words.

"We pause now for station identification," Latham said, and a woman in a housedress and immaculately groomed hair asked a druggist in a white coat what laxative she should choose. "For occasional irregularity." The druggist had the answer on the tip of his tongue. It was the one most doctors recommended. "Yes, seven out of ten doctors in a nationwide survey recommend this gentle but reliable product for—"

"After all, it's Saturday and it's summer," Janet said. "Nothing much happens on a summer—"

"Search planes have spotted what is believed to be the wreckage of a chartered flight with eighty persons aboard in a mountainous area some ten miles from the Munich airport," Latham said. "The plane, which disappeared from radar screens in the early morning hours, was bound for Yugoslavia, with a stop scheduled at Munich. The flight originated in Amsterdam. No Americans are believed to have been aboard. A sharp increase in employment is reported from Spokane, Washington. We switch now to the IBC correspondent in Spokane, Robert Wells."

"This is Robert Wells, reporting for the Independent Broadcasting Company from Spokane, Washington. All indices here point to a sharp upturn in employment since last spring's near recession. According to the president of the Chamber of Commerce, conditions in the labor market have—"

Sitting beside Janet on the Streeters' terrace, Clay Carter interrupted Robert Wells. He interrupted Wells by saying "Damn!" not loudly, but with an explosion in the word. Janet looked at him. "Oh," Clay said, "you ought to know a goddamn handout when you hear it, girl. Wells is on tape. Latham had no business using it, if Wells fell flat on his ass."

"And now," in a new voice from the little set, "for Ronald Latham's commentary on today's news. But first a brief pause for this message."

The message was delivered, graphically, by the picture of a sleek jet plane flying above clouds. By voice: "Fly East-West Airways. The world's most accomplished airline. Hourly departures for Chicago and other points. For reservations, consult your travel agent."

"A somewhat unfortunate coin—" Paul Streeter said, stooping to pick up Carter's glass from the flagstones. He broke the sentence there because the little TV set intervened.

"And now, Ronald Latham's thoughts on the news of this Saturday." Mr. Latham's transformation from reporter to, presumably, seer, had made no change in his appearance, except he seemed slightly dimmer. ("Damn battery," Clay said.)

"All administrations exhibit euphoria when discussing their actions and predicting the new heights of national well-being which will result from those actions," Latham said, looking intently at the camera—or possibly at the prompter. "This Administration is no exception. Its euphoria has not always, perhaps, seemed entirely justified, particularly to leading Democrats, whose views we have just heard Senator Perkins set forth so cogently.

"But much of today's news would seem to justify the optimism of Administration spokesmen. The sharp rise in employment on the West Coast will appear to many a most promising sign of expanding economy. And the upward trend of the major industrial indices, while not statistically large, is encouraging indication that the President's economic policies, so often derided by his critics in the Congress and elsewhere, are having—are, at the least, beginning to have—the salutary effect on the nation's economy of which Administration spokesmen have all along been confident. Probably, if improvement on the West Coast is to be weighed at its full value, the ensuing months may see a sharp drop in the current rate of unemployment.

"Various factors may, of course, hamper the Administration's progress toward its desired goal. Sharp cuts in the nation's defense budget, such as are advocated by Senator Perkins and others, might seriously affect the expected gain in employment. The passage, possibly over Presidential veto, of utopian social legislation, might well disrupt the economy and result in even more disastrous inflation. And probable excessive demands by big labor may, as so often in the past, have adverse effects on economic stability. All these elements must be taken into account as we look toward the future.

"But today's events promise—"

Clayton Carter turned a knob. The set whined for an instant and fell dark and silent.

"A bit out of step, isn't he?" Streeter said. He had been standing, listening, with Clay's empty glass in his hand.

"Well," Clay said, "he sure as hell hears a different drum."

"Yes," Streeter said. "I thought you more or less set the beat. Gin and tonic?"

"A martini this time around," Clay said. "If you don't mind. And go easy on the arsenic, Paul."

As Streeter walked away toward the bar, Clay reached out and turned the TV set on again. The screen was noticeably dimmer and the sound more faint. "Battery's about dead," Carter said to nobody in particular. "And that is the news this Saturday night," Latham whispered, and shuffled papers together and vanished. The next whisper was that of the announcer.

"IBC's 'The News Tonight' comes to you at this

hour six days a week, Monday through Friday with Clayton Carter, and Saturday with—"

The sound faded out entirely.

"Perhaps batteries know best," Carter said, and this time spoke to Janet, who said, "Well, he's your boy, Clay. You decided to try him out. And to let him make his comment."

"I know," Clay said. "Mea culpa."

"The editorial's a new twist," she said. "You don't editorialize yourself." She paused for a moment. "Directly," she added.

"He wanted a shot at it," Clay told her. "And things do tend to be dull on Saturdays. So, call it an experiment. And we'll give him Z for effort."

"The Administration," Janet said, "will give him B-plus. A, maybe."

Clayton Carter said, "Yeah," and looked away at the green hills. Now only the tops of trees on the hill summits had sun on them. Then he took the gimmick off the table and put it on the terrace floor and said, "Thanks, Paul," for a martini in a chilled glass. Streeter said, "Mmmm," and started away.

"By the way," Clay said, and Paul Streeter stopped to listen. "Some place handy I can plug this in for a while? Battery's gone dead."

"Socket up there," Streeter said, and pointed. "Cap on it, but it's less than ten feet from the pool. Violation of some code or law or something, but that's where it was when we bought the place. Help yourself."

Clay carried the set in the direction Streeter had indicated, found an electric outlet in a stubby post and plugged the set in. A small red light went on in the top of the little set, unexpectedly visible in the growing duskiness of the terrace. He came back to his drink and to Janet. Nora Curran had moved from her chair next to Janet's and was sitting now beside Agnes Streeter. The so-very-red-haired man had gone to the bar end of the terrace and was watching Paul Streeter pouring charcoal briquets into the bowl of a broiler. Paul laid an electric started on top of the charcoal in the broiler and poured more briquets over it. He plugged the starter in.

The maid brought more hot canapés from the house and passed them. Paul made new drinks. Smoke began to drift up from the broiler; it whispered away from those on the terrace. Paul distributed drinks where they were needed or at any rate, acceptable.

Janet accepted a fresh martini, wondering vaguely whether she really needed it. She looked up at Paul and smiled at him and thought, The mind plays foolish tricks. Why did I get the notion I'd seen him somewhere before today? She said, "Thank you, Paul." She watched Clay finish his drink and, in response to Paul's lifted eyebrows, hold the empty glass out to him. She watched Paul carry the glass toward the bar.

"It's pleasant here," she said. "I'm so glad the Streeters—"

She stopped, because Clay spoke at the same time, looking away from the hills and toward her. Words tangled between them.

"People—I'm sorry. You were saying something."

"Only that it's nice here. People what, Clay?"

"Change," Clayton Carter said. "Not a very profound thought. And it is nice here. Relaxing. And Paul asked me if I knew how you liked your steak and I said I thought rare. All right?"

"Yes," she said. "Who changes, Clay? The Streeters?"

"I suppose so," Clay said. "Coming into what looks like being a good deal of money does change people."

"From an aunt, Dr. Streeter says. Defunct aunt, of course."

Clay Carter said, "Mmmm." He said, "I wasn't thinking about the Streeters. About Latham. I knew him years ago. In Washington at first. Then we were both in Saigon. At the start—near the start—of that mess there. Worked for the Bishop chain. A good reporter, Ron Latham was. Knew a hopeless mess when he saw one and filed what he saw. His papers used what they thought suitable. We saw a bit of each other. Had drinks together and cried into them about the prevailing idiocy."

"When you were writing for *Manhattan*," she said. "And I was just starting in college and reading you. You were making it clear enough it was a hopeless mess."

"Magazines—those like *Manhattan* anyway—are one thing," he said. "Newspapers are another. Not that the Bishop outfit isn't pretty good. They went along with Latham a good deal of the time. He wasn't the Latham we heard tonight. That Wells tape—it's been around since Thursday. I'd no idea Latham was going to dig it up and use it as a lead-in for that Washington Knows Best crap. The hell of it is I O.K.'d Ron when it leaked out he'd just as soon switch networks. Told Willis I thought he'd be a good man. G.W.'s idea in the first place. I'll give myself that much."

"God Wills," Janet said, using the alternative, and unpublicized, version of Godfrey Willis's initials—a version possibly unknown to the program vice-president of IBC.

"Naughty," Clay said, with no conviction in his

voice. "Our greatly admired chief, my dear. Yes, Latham's God Willis's boy. But I didn't buck it. Remembered the good guy I knew in Saigon."

"And now?"

"Monday I'll buck it," Clay said. "All the way up the line if I have to."

"A lot of the affiliates will lap him up," Janet said. "Which may have been in Mr. Willis's mind, Clay."

Carter said, "Mmmm." He lifted his head a little and sniffed the air. He said, "Smells good."

Broiling steaks smell good at any time, but best of all when carried on soft summer air on a country terrace.

They ate on the terrace, each from the little table beside him. Paul Streeter had a way with steaks. The steak knives the Streeters provided for their guests glided through the meat. And the steaks were rare under the char of the surfaces.

3

PAUL STREETER SWITCHED OFF the floodlights after Mabel had cleared the little tables. He left a soft light burning on the bar and served coffee from there. He offered liqueurs and had no takers. Charcoal still glowed in the grill and, at the other end of the terrace, a small red light showed on Clay Carter's gimmick, patiently charging its battery. Cigarette tips pulsed in the semi-darkness and people talked. Or didn't talk. It is very peaceful here, Janet thought. Half a moon was up, whitening the distant hills.

It was a few minutes after ten when Clay, beside her, said, "Well, lady?"

"I'd think so," Janet said, and swung long legs off the chaise. Agnes Streeter told everybody that it was early yet. She told them that, after all, it was a Saturday night. But Bernard Simmons stood up and rubbed his cigarette out in the tray, and reached a hand down to Nora Curran on the chaise beside him. She took the hand which, Janet was sure, she by no means needed. Nora told her hosts it had been a lovely party, and the others made "Mmmms!" of agreement. Janet said, "Wonderful steaks, Paul," and everybody said, "Mmmm!" again. Agnes said, "I wish you wouldn't. You'd better turn the lights on, Paul."

They went back into the house, and Nora and Janet Osborne went up the stairs to the rooms they had changed in. Janet's tennis dress, which she had stretched on a chair by an open window, was almost dry when she folded it into the small suitcase with the tennis shoes. She strapped her racket to the case.

Nora Curran came along the corridor, carrying her racket in one hand and what appeared to be a briefcase in the other. They went down the wide staircase side by side, and Agnes Streeter was waiting at the foot of it. She said, "Paul's just making sure about the fire. He's fussy about fires."

Nora told her that fires were good things to be fussy about, and Clay and the red-haired man came along the hallway from the back of the house. Seen in the light again, Assistant District Attorney Bernard Simmons's hair was just as surprisingly red as Janet had remembered it.

Agnes touched a switch, and light flooded down on the turnaround in front of the house and the two cars waiting there. Agnes said, "I can't think what's keeping —oh, here he is."

They were out on the driveway gravel by then. Paul Streeter came around a corner of the house. He had a flashlight in his left hand and Carter's very portable little gimmick in his right. The beam from the flashlight was absorbed in the light streaming down from above, and Streeter switched the flashlight off.

"Didn't want you to forget it," Streeter said, and lifted the TV set a little to identify the "it."

"Thanks," Clay said, "not that I would have," and reached out for the gimmick. He reached with a hand already holding Janet's case and racket and was told that he already had his hands full.

They walked to the cars and said, again, the things they had said on the terrace and shook hands. Paul's hand was thin and hard in Janet's. But his brief grip was gentle. He looked at her, she thought, intently, as if he were trying to remember her.

There was a little traffic on the Saw Mill going in. Not many head toward the city's breathlessness on Saturday nights. Clay drove fast. At Ninety-sixth Street he turned off the Henry Hudson Parkway.

Janet said, "But—"

"Small detour," Clay said. "You've never seen my house. And it's not really all that late. Of course, if you think it is—" He slowed the car. "It's easy enough to swing back around."

"I'd love to see your house," Janet said, and was told she was a good girl and that he would even buy her a drink. He turned the car up Riverside Drive. He drove north for half a dozen blocks, with apartment houses on one side and a strip of park on the other. He pulled into the curb.

The house he stopped in front of was narrow and tall. It seemed to stand in a clearing. Much taller and wider apartment buildings rose on either side of it, but each stood away from the house, beyond a narrow strip of lawn. There were, of course, brown patches in the grass on either side of the narrow house. Janet rolled down the window, and warm air came into the car. She merely looked at the narrow house, which seemed to shrink away, shrink inward, from the buildings beside it.

"You're supposed to say something," Clay said. " 'Good God,' or '*Je*sus Christ.' Or just, 'I don't believe it.' People do, first time around."

Still looking at the narrow house, Janet said, "It is—well, unexpected."

"Z for effort, Janet," Clay said. "I hoped for better. It's a relic, girl. Of another age. My grandfather's age, actually. Come on."

He had got out of the car and come around it. He opened the door for her.

"We should have arrived in a carriage," Clay said. "Or at least a hansom. Grandfather did, I suppose."

He touched her arm, guiding her toward the door of the house, which stood flush with the sidewalk. There were four white steps up to the door. There was a polished brass handrail. He unlocked the door and they went into a narrow entrance hall, with a narrow staircase rising along one side of it. The stairs had a polished rail of dark wood. There were closed double doors in the wall opposite the staircase. Carter pushed them open and flicked a switch beyond them. Light glowed from four big table lamps in a long narrow room. Logs were arranged neatly in the fireplace. Deep sofas—low, modern sofas—faced each other beside the fireplace. There was a wide rectangular table between the sofas.

It was pleasantly cool in the long narrow room; there was the subdued hum of air conditioning at work. Clay guided her to one of the sofas, and she looked down the softly lighted room. She said, "Clay, it's lovely."

There was a strange sound from the far end of the room. It was between a snarl and a baby's scream.

"Just Mao, by way of greeting," Clay said. "Hello, yourself, cat."

A long, slender cat, with a dark brown face and stockings and tail of the same brown, came up the room—came halfway up the room and floated up onto an end table. He spoke, in slightly softer tones than before, and put his forepaws meticulously together and sat tall. His body was the color of coffee with much cream in it.

"Yes," Clay said, "you're a very handsome cat. We're both looking at you."

The Siamese said nothing. He looked fixedly at Janet Osborne. The gaze made her feel slightly self-conscious, as if she were failing to do something expected of her.

"The promised drink," Clay said. "A cognac?"

"Fine," Janet said. "I feel like a bird being hypnotized."

"His idea, probably," Carter said. "Not that we have much notion what their ideas are. Do cats bother you? If they do, I'll tell him to get out."

"They don't bother me. He's a very beautiful cat. You mean if you told him to get out he would?"

"No, of course not. And if I carry him out he'll yell bloody murder. Won't you, Mao?"

Mao looked at Clay Carter. Mao said, "Yahr-ah."

Carter walked over to Mao and scratched him behind his pointed dark brown ears. A resonant humming sound came from the cat.

"He has a very loud purr," Carter said. "He's all in all a very loud cat. Runs in the family pretty much."

Mao said, "Oh-*ower*," in two syllables. Carter walked down to the end of the room and pushed on something, and a door of a cabinet built into the wall opened. He took a bottle out of the cabinet and poured from it into two small glasses. He brought the glasses back up the room and put them on the wide table. He sat on the other deep sofa. He lifted his glass and she raised hers, and the glasses clicked between them.

"You were tactful about Paul's backhand," he told her.

"You told me to be. He takes tennis seriously, doesn't he?"

"He takes most things seriously," Clay said. "He's had a serious life, from what I know of it."

"Oh?"

"Worked his way through college in California, according to a profile the *Chronicle* ran about him a few years back. Sold encyclopedias, for all I know. Worked in filling stations, as I remember it. Repaired radios. Got his master's while he was an instructor. Still an instructor when he got his doctorate. A very serious young man. Diligent. Speaking of the *Chronicle*—"

"We weren't, Clay. We've been over it—for now, anyway. Then radio and television on the West Coast. Then Dyckman. That's what you said, wasn't it?"

"Yes. Are you really all this much interested in Paul Streeter?"

"No, not really. Only, when I first saw him this afternoon I felt I'd seen him somewhere before. Just— oh, one of those vague things. I thought maybe if I knew more about him it would come back to me."

"Out of the fog," Clay said. "I know. Irritating to half remember a half memory. About all I know about Paul. Except he's a nice guy and broils a good steak. And is on the same side of things I am. Damn Latham. Damn God Wills, for that matter. I let my guard down badly, girl."

"He wasn't all that bad," Janet said. "They come worse."

"Not on IBC, as long as I have a say. And my stock has a say."

"Just giving the Administration a break," Janet said, and got a pack of cigarettes out of her handbag. Clay lighted her cigarette. "The fairness doctrine." Janet spoke through a haze of exhaled smoke.

He told her what could be done with the fairness doctrine. "Remember Hemingway's dodge?" he said. She shook her head. " 'Obscenity Naples.' Or maybe it was Florence. Seemed like rather a large order. You missed his inflections."

She shook her head again.

"Latham's," he said. "Probably you were just a tot when Bill Shirer was broadcasting from Berlin."

"I was never a tot. I wouldn't have stood for it."

"I sit corrected," Clay said. "We need another drink."

She put fingers over her glass.

The cat Mao came down from his table with the softest of thuds. He said, "Wow-*ar*," in less strident voice. He walked over and smelled Janet's shoes. He smelled both of them very carefully.

"Was feeling left out," Clay said. "They don't like that."

Clay reached a hand down to Mao. Mao smelled the proffered hand briefly. He returned to Janet's shoes. "Knows me, just investigating you," Clay said. "Think she'll do, Mao?" Mao looked up at Clay Carter. Mao said, "Mrow," speaking softly for a Siamese. Then he began to purr.

"Yes, I think so too," Carter said, and went down the long narrow room. He came back with a bottle of

Martell cognac. He put the bottle on the table and looked across the table at Janet and said, "Sure?"

"Perhaps a drop," she said, and he poured into her glass. "Someone called Shirer?"

"A network man in Berlin. Hell, it was before the war. You wouldn't even have started to be a tot. I was pretty much a kid myself. Probably my father had me listen. Probably told me what to listen for."

He sipped from his glass.

"You get to thinking you remember things you've only been told about. You wouldn't know that yet. Shirer broadcast on shortwave, of course. Censored to hell and gone, naturally. But they couldn't censor his tone of voice. A typescript can look cold and innocent, even to Hitler's boys. Voice inflections—well, they can change a lot. Skepticism can seep in. Even derision. And some words in American English have connotations which could escape men taught English in German schools. All right, I could have read Latham's bit tonight—well, so it would have had a different impact."

"Which some people would call 'slanting,' " Janet said and sipped from her glass.

"Everything that passes through a human mind is slanted," Clay said, "by the contours of that mind. By all the past and present of that mind. By everything that has happened to it. Objectivity-shibbolethity."

"There's no such word," Janet told him.

"There is now. I just made it up."

She blew smoke into the air and looked at it. A current of air took the smoke away.

"This house is something that happened to you, isn't it, Clay? You grew up here?"

"Until I went to prep school."

"With carriages drawing up to the door."

Carter smiled and shook his head. "My father had

a horseless carriage," he told her, with gravity in his voice. "A late-model Chalmers, I think it was. Or a Stanley Steamer, perhaps."

She shook her head slowly, in evident bewilderment. This time he laughed, not loudly.

"Antiques, child. Even before my time. Dad had Buicks, actually. Cadillacs, later on."

"Buicks," she said. "Cadillacs. Prep schools. Then what? Harvard?"

"Princeton."

"And this town house to grow up in. How old is this house, Clay?"

"A hundred and fifty years. Give or take."

"Why here?"

It was his turn to shake an uncomprehending head.

"Riverside Drive. Why not the Upper East Side? Sutton Place?"

"Oh. Riverside Drive was a good address when Grandfather Carter bought this house. To-hell-and-gone uptown, of course. Private houses like this. Some big enough to be called mansions. You could still see the river in those days, I suppose. When you could still see through the air. Things were moving east when my father was a young man. But Sutton Place hadn't really been invented."

"What's happened to a mind puts contours into it, you said. You were for McGovern."

"Not on the air. Impartial on the air. Not what the Administration wants. What it got. About contours: one generation's ridges may turn into the next generation's hollows. Didn't you tell me your father voted for Goldwater?"

"All right."

"And you're the faithful assistant of Clayton Carter, font of elitist gossip. To say nothing of liberal plugola—sorry. 'So-called' liberal plugola. To say nothing of your to-be-deplored association with one Philip Whitmore. Where is he now, by the way? Not in New York, I take it."

"Why? Oh, all right. Because I was free this afternoon. That's what you mean."

Clay Carter said he supposed so.

"Phil's in Paris. Or on his way back from Paris."

"For the *Chronicle?*"

She put her glass down on the table with a click. There was still a little brandy in the glass. She moved in the deep sofa, preliminary to getting up from it.

"All right," Clay said. "You're quite safe with me, Miss Osborne. Finish your drink. We won't talk about Mr. Whitmore. Tonight, I mean—I won't say I won't bring the matter up again. Until you tell me, once and for all, that you're—well, fed to the teeth with the whole subject."

Suddenly she leaned forward and put her hands over her eyes. When she spoke, her voice was very low and shook a little. "Damn it all, Clay, why can't you leave me alone? Just leave me *alone!*"

"Is that really the way you want it?"

Still with her hands covering her eyes, she moved her head slowly from side to side. He waited. It seemed to him that it was minutes before she spoke again, and then her voice was muffled.

"I don't know," she said. "Can't you get it through your head I don't *know?* Can't you leave me alone?"

"All right, can Phil? Leave you alone, I mean."

She took her hands down from her face and sat straight in the chair. "Not your business, is it? Why don't you go back to your wife, Clay?"

"You've got it mixed up, my dear. It was the other

way round. It was Grace who took off. I told you that when—when the subject first came up. When—"

"When you first suggested we sleep together."

The words were hard, precise. But there was no hardness in her voice. "Quit sleeping with Phil and start sleeping with my boss."

"No, girl. It's not like that. And you know it. Sleeping with Clay Carter. Sure. Not with something called a 'boss.'"

"All right. I'm sorry I put it that way. Clay Carter wants to sleep with Janet Osborne." Suddenly her lips curved into a smile. "Person to person," she added.

The tension which had grown between them vanished suddenly. He smiled back at her.

"Sleeping would be incidental," he said. "An afterthought."

He got up from his chair and leaned down to kiss her. After a moment, her lips responded to his. For an instant she held his face in both her hands. Then, gently, she pushed him away.

"And Jannie can't make her mind up," she said, lightness in her voice. "She can't say no. She can't say yes." She looked up at him. "You'll have to let me work it out," she said. "And now you'd better take me home, I think. Or call a cab."

He stood straight and reached down for his glass. He emptied it. "Lady," he said, "this is New York. You don't call cabs in New York. You field them. And not on Riverside Drive at"—he looked at the watch on his wrist—"almost midnight."

As she stood up, there was a light thump on the floor. Mao came down from a table with a lamp on it. He certainly liked tables. He said "Wow-ow" in a discontented tone. He undulated to Janet and began to rub against her ankles. He also began to purr. When she moved one foot, he moved inches away from it and looked up at her. He said "Wow-ahhr" in a voice louder than before.

"All right, Mao, I don't want her to either," Clay said. "But we'll just have to humor the lady."

Mao looked up at Clay and said "Wow-ahhr" again. He was quite testy about it.

They made it to the door without stepping on the Siamese cat, a success to which the cat contributed nothing. But he stopped in the entrance hall and glared at the front door. He also spoke to it.

"I'll be back," Clay Carter said, as he followed Janet out of the house. "And don't go waking Cyril up."

It was warm outside the house. The air was humid, weighed on them. Janet said, "Cyril?" as they crossed the sidewalk toward the car.

"Cyril Johnson," Clay said. "Takes care of me and the house and the pool."

She stopped so abruptly that he bumped into her. She said, "Pool? You mean *swimming* pool? Here? A *private* swimming pool?"

"This was almost country when Grandfather bought the house," Clay said. "The pool was already behind the house when he bought it. Dad had it modernized. Filter and that sort of thing. All right, it's an anomaly. But it's there."

Janet said, "Good God," as she got into the car. They circled back to the Henry Hudson. There was little southbound traffic on it, or on the West Side Highway. It took less than fifteen minutes to reach the Nineteenth Street turnoff. Parked trucks were somnolent at the curbs. Half an hour after they had left the narrow house on Riverside, Clay pulled to the curb in front of a not dissimilar house in Waverly Place, except that this house stood shoulder to shoulder with others like it.

He got out and came around the car and opened the door for her. They went up five worn brownstone steps together. She unlocked the outside door and held it open but then turned to him.

"You wanted to know whether Phil is leaving me alone. In the way you mean it, Clay, the answer is yes. We're—well, we're leaving each other alone. Until I work things out. Good night, Clay."

He said, "We're both patient men. Good night, my dear."

She went into the dimly lighted vestibule and he went back to the car. He did not start it until lights went on behind the second-floor windows, which was where her apartment was. Then he drove back uptown. He took the gimmick out of the car and carried it into the house.

Mao was glad to see him; Mao resented the fact that Clay went to the telephone before he sat down to provide a lap. He objected to the fact that Clay, after he had sat down, poured a nightcap into his little glass. Finally, the lap was ready and Mao purred his way onto it. He interrupted his resonant purr only briefly when the garageman sounded the horn twice to indicate that the car had been picked up as ordered.

4

SHE WAS ON HER THIRD cup of coffee and the day's first cigarette when the telephone rang. She was sitting in the living room of the floor-through apartment, wearing the lightest of robes, and the window air conditioner was humming. (It wasn't, so far as she could tell, doing much of anything else.) She looked at her watch as she walked across the room. It was a little after ten. It was also Sunday morning. Something of "It's a little after ten on a Sunday morning" was in her voice as she said "Yes?" to the telephone.

"You sound grouchy," Philip Whitmore told her. "It's not all that early. Or were you up all that late?"

"Hello, Phil," Janet said, and felt a momentary tightness closing in. Yet also she was glad to hear the familiar deep voice. "I thought you were in Paris."

"Got in around noon yesterday," he said. "Rang you as soon as I got home. No Jan. Out gallivanting.

With the Voice. You can't keep things from the press, honey chile."

Philip Whitmore had been born in Georgia. Now and then he made a point of it.

"Nothing to keep," she said. "Clay took me up to some friends of his in Westchester. We played tennis and had dinner. You want it in the form of an affidavit?"

"Grumpy," he said. "To Dr. and Mrs. Streeter's. Carter's secretary is all-knowing."

"They like to know where to reach him," Janet said. "Miss Dawes isn't supposed to broadcast. Did you just call up to wrangle, dear?" The "dear" was somewhat unexpected to herself.

"That's more like it," Phil said. "No. To ask you out to dinner. So that I can regale you with an account of my ten days in Paris for the New York *Chronicle,* the world's newspaper of record."

"Tonight?"

"Unless you're hopelessly tied up. Unless—?"

He did not need to add to the last "unless?" They both push, she thought. They both pull, she thought. Things were so simple before I went to work with Clay.

"I'd love to," Janet Osborne heard herself say. And, yes, seven would be fine. She heard "Until seven then, darling," and the click of a replaced telephone.

Probably I'm a damn fool, she thought. Probably I want to be pulled at and pushed at. Probably I'm flattered. Sometimes I'm discouraged with myself. I should get me to a nunnery. But I'd hate a nunnery. I'd be miserable in a nunnery. Damn!

The coffee was cold in her cup. It also was cold in the Chemex. She made herself fresh coffee. She had a fresh cigarette with her fresh coffee.

All right, she was looking forward to seeing Phil Whitmore at seven. And to seeing Clay Carter at ten tomorrow morning. All right, I enjoy being a woman disputed. Probably I'm a floozy by nature. An incipient one, anyway. It's going to be another stiflingly hot day. Maybe what I really need is a cold shower.

She did not take a cold shower. She lugged up the Sunday edition of the New York *Chronicle,* a heap in the entrance vestibule. She had to put on slacks and shirt to go down for it.

Philip Whitmore's opposite-editorial-page column was datelined Paris. The French were disenchanted with American economic policy, as dictated by the White House. Their view of the Administration in Washington was dim and growing dimmer. This was not bluntly said. Bluntness, never notably a characteristic of the French, had been curbed since De Gaulle. But suspicion and distrust of American intentions, of American maturity, were between the lines—to be heard in the inflections of important voices. "The shadow of Vietnam still lies over the United States," Philip Whitmore wrote. "It may be years before it is dissipated, if it is ever dissipated. It is not French to say, 'We told you so.' It is only human to imply it."

Phil Whitmore had been one of the many American correspondents to see future disaster in South Vietnam. Clayton Carter had been another. And Ronald Latham, according to Clay, had been one more. Washington had preferred to listen to Joseph Alsop. It was water under the bridge now—water with bodies floating in it.

At twelve-thirty, and with a slight feeling of disloyalty, Janet got "Face the Nation" on television. She made herself a small martini to go with it. The wrong channel, of course. The wrong network. A Democratic senator, under questioning, lamented the usurpation of power by the White House. He could not speak for the House. He felt a growing determination in the Senate to reassume its constitutionally imposed responsibilities.

"On another subject, Senator, do you expect any Senate reaction to what many see as an implied threat by this Administration to discipline the broadcasting industry? In other words, to compel reporting that is uniformly favorable to Administration positions?"

Many senators, including the one being interviewed, had been disquieted by the statements of some White House spokesmen. The Senator quoted Thomas Jefferson on the necessity of a free press. He noted the existence of the First Amendment. He was thanked, and excused.

So many people on our side, Janet thought, as she turned a knob and, after a gulp or two, got silence. And something called Bartwell Industries swallows the publishing house that nice Nora Curran works for. As a chaser to a corporation that makes ships for the Navy. Of course, CBS swallowed Holt, Rinehart and Winston and RCA absorbed Random House. But they're networks and in communications, too. In the use of words, anyway. I wonder if Bartwell Industries really does make paper clips? Will I let Phil sleep with me tonight? After all these months? And if I don't will it be because of what I implied to Clay last night? And am I really the shapeless mess I seem to myself today?

She made herself a crab-meat salad. She went out, briefly, and walked in Washington Square. There were people from out of town in the Square, people with cameras. They took pictures of each other. There were a boy with a guitar and two other boys and two girls to sing with him. The boys had beards and the girls didn't. On the other hand, the girls had just perceptible breasts. A policeman in a short-sleeved blue shirt watched them with no particular interest. He took his uniform cap off and rubbed sweat off his forehead with the palm of his right hand. He put the cap back on again. The singing wasn't very good. Anyway, it was too hot in the Square. It was even more smotheringly hot than it had been yesterday. The Streeters were lucky to live in the country; lucky to have inherited from a rich aunt.

Back in her apartment it felt cool at first. But then the coolness ebbed away. It had been only the illusion of coolness.

She took her clothes off and stretched on her bed beside the humming air conditioner. It was a double bed. More than a year ago she had bought it to replace a narrow bed. Phil had a beard then and I didn't like it and he shaved it off.

She slept. In a dream there was, walking down a corridor, a man she at first thought was Paul Streeter. But when he walked closer she saw that it was not Streeter but a man she had never seen before. He was, however, carrying a tennis racket.

She was ready at ten minutes of seven. Phil was likely to be prompt; he had spent most of his life meeting deadlines. She had showered, ending with cold water. She had put on a sleeveless mint-green dress and put a white evening purse handy to pick up. She had put white gloves beside the purse. She had straightened up the apartment and made the bed up neatly. To show it was not available for use? She had turned the controls on the air conditioners in the living-room and bedroom windows to "Cooler"—as far as they would go. She had filled the ice bucket and set out stemmed glasses, on the chance they would have a drink before they went to a restaurant.

She was ready. But for what am I ready? It was simple before I went to IBC and met Clay there and began to see what was in Clay Carter's eyes. Phil and I were all right for each other. Were we more than just all right? I didn't wonder about that a year ago. It hadn't become something I had to work out—had to consider and wonder about. There wasn't any confusion in my mind a year ago. And Phil shaved off his beard because I asked him to.

The buzzer sounded. She had been waiting for the buzzer, but all the same its sound made her jump. I'm coming to pieces, she thought, as she pressed the button and went to open the apartment door. She stood in the doorway and watched Philip Whitmore come up the stairs, as for almost two years she had so often watched.

He had not changed. Why on earth would he have changed in a little over two weeks? Why did I think, He hasn't changed? I'm really falling apart. "Hi, Phil." Is there a flatness in my voice? Or welcome in it?

Philip Whitmore was an inch or so under six feet. He had very black hair. He had not been out in the sun much. The games Phil Whitmore played were played at a typewriter, were played at Washington cocktail parties, were played over drinks at restaurant tables. But he came up the stairs like the athlete he was not. When he said, "Hi, Jan," there was no doubt about the quality of his voice. He put his arms around her in the doorway, and his lips on hers.

But his lips left hers quickly. He drew back a little and looked at her. He said, "So?" and they went into the apartment, one of his lean arms lightly about her shoulders. He closed the door after them.

"You don't learn, do you?" he said. "I keep telling you, but you don't learn. You're supposed to call down before you buzz in. I might have been Jack the Ripper."

"I didn't have a date with Jack the Ripper," she said. "You haven't let the beard grow back." (Which, she thought, was a ridiculous thing to have said.)

He laughed lightly. (Nobody else laughs in quite the way he does.)

"Biding my time on the beard," he said. "How's Clay? As if I give a damn."

"Clay's all right," she said. "Shall we have a drink here? Or wait until we get to the restaurant?"

"The restaurant," he said. "Since I gather one thing's not going to lead to another. Hugo's? Since it's near. And open, which is something of an advantage. We'll have a nightcap here when we come back."

She said, "Fine," and picked up her purse and gloves. She put the gloves on and he watched her. He shook his head slowly.

"It was eighty-nine an hour ago," he said.

"They keep hands clean," she told him. She led the way down the stairs. On the sidewalk the air was still and hot—quite unnecessarily hot.

There was a cab just passing the house. Its top light was on and Whitmore yelled at it. It pulled to the curb. "But it's only a few—" Janet said. "Oh, all right."

"Never look a gift taxi in the face," Phil said, and they got into the cab which, rather miraculously, was air-conditioned.

It was, of course, only a few blocks to Hugo's French Restaurant. The cabbie had hoped for better things. But his, "Thank you, Mac," was cordial. (He must have overtipped, Janet thought.)

There was plenty of room at the bar. One of the

half-dozen people sitting at it was a noticeably thin man with noticeably red hair. Another of them, beside him, was Nora Curran. Bernard Simmons looked at them as they sat down, and Janet nodded and smiled.

Phil Whitmore said, "Hi, Counselor," and Simmons said, "Evening, Seer. Miss Osborne. Why don't you two—"

But he did not finish, because the maître d' came to the bar and leaned down and said something to the red-haired man.

Assistant District Attorney Bernard Simmons said, "Damn!" and looked at the girl sitting beside him and shook his head. Then he got up and followed the maître d'.

Nora Curran said something to the glass in front of her. Her voice was very low, and there seemed to be resignation in her tone. I can guess the word, Janet thought.

"A very dry martini, please," she said to the barman. "With a twist."

"Same," Phil Whitmore said. "And House of Lords, please."

The barman scooped crushed ice into stemmed glasses. He mixed martinis. They lifted glasses and clicked them together.

They were halfway down their drinks, and Phil was eating peanuts, when Janet felt rather than saw Nora Curran's movement. Nora slid off her chair and stood beside it and looked down into the restaurant. Janet looked with her.

Bernard Simmons was walking toward the bar. As he walked, he moved his head slowly from side to side. Janet looked at the slender girl in a white dress for whom the shaken head was clearly meant. She saw Nora's shoulders lift a little and fall again, resignation in the movement.

Simmons did not look at them. He did not sit down again at the bar. He reached and picked up his half-empty glass and emptied it.

"Damn telephones," Nora said, quite clearly. "Damn Alexander Graham Bell, for that matter."

Simmons patted one of her shoulders gently, obviously in consolation. He put four dollar bills on the bar and flicked a hand in answer to the barman's "Thank you, sir."

Simmons and Nora Curran went out of the restaurant, she talking to him and he smiling down at her and shaking his head slowly—rather dolefully, Janet thought.

"Probably somebody's killed somebody," Philip Whitmore said, and finished what remained in his cocktail glass. "Simmons likes to be in on the ground floor. Acts as if he were a cop himself, they say. Seemed to know you, Jan."

"He was at the Streeters' last night," Janet said. "In the District Attorney's office, isn't he?"

"Deputy chief, Homicide Bureau," Whitmore told her, and signaled to the barman, who scooped crushed ice into fresh glasses and stirred fresh martinis. He did not measure gin or vermouth. When he poured, he precisely filled both glasses.

The maître d' brought big menu cards to them when their glasses were half emptied. They ordered, finished their drinks, followed the maître d' to a table in an alcove. The alcove gave seclusion. Phil Whitmore ordered another drink from the waiter captain, but Janet shook her head to his lifted eyebrows.

The food was all right.

"Not quite as good food as Charles used to have," Phil said. "Do you remember Charles? Remember the *pot-au-feu*?"

Of course she remembered Charles Restaurant, which had been a block up the avenue. She also remembered the *pot-au-feu* and the camaraderie at the bar.

Phil said, "Pity. Some things ought to last forever." He paused and looked at his plate. He said, "All right, Jan. May as well get it over. What's with you and Clay Carter?"

She had known it was coming. The air between them had vibrated with it since he had walked up the stairs in Waverly Place. It had been between their lips when he had kissed her in the doorway of the apartment and her lips had not responded.

She looked down at her emptied plate; she sipped water she did not want from her glass. She said, "Nothing," in a very low voice, and spoke to her empty plate.

"No," Phil said. "Not good enough, dear. Look at me, Jan."

She looked at him. "All right," she said. "I don't know. Is that good enough?"

"No. And don't, for God's sake, tell me it's none of my business."

"I wasn't going to. You know I wasn't going to. You know I don't—just write things off. You ought to know it, anyway. There is nothing with Clay and me. Probably there never will be. In the way you mean it."

"In the way we both mean it, Jan. And, I suppose, the way he means it. Do you ever look at yourself in the mirror, honey? Or, for that matter, look into your own mind? Or even listen to your own voice? Clay's no fool. Neither am I, come to that."

She said, "Give me a cigarette, Phil." He gave her a cigarette and lighted it. She took another sip of water she didn't want.

"We've got to talk about it," he said. "It won't just drift away, you know."

"I know," she said. "I know it won't. But not here. Maybe not tonight."

"Tonight."

"When we get back to the apartment, then. Order us coffee, Phil."

He ordered them coffee.

It was a little cooler with the sun finally down for the night. They walked the few blocks back to the apartment in Waverly Place. They walked in silence. When they stepped down from the curb at Eighth Street, Phil took her arm and held her back. She had not, he thought, really seen the taxicab she had been about to walk in front of.

When they were safe across Eighth, she said, "Thank you, Phil," in a voice so low he could just hear it.

In the reasonably cool apartment, she said, "You know where things are. Do you mind? We're almost missing the news."

It was just after nine. A weekend roundup of news at nine o'clock on Sunday evenings was a new experiment of Clayton Carter's. The first ratings hadn't been too bad—not for Sunday evenings in the summer. She turned a knob.

The newscaster, when he came on, was not Ronald Latham, as she had supposed it would be, since the man who did the Saturday night news usually was anchorman on Sundays. The man giving the news had rather long yellowish hair and, somewhat unexpectedly, wore a white shirt and a dark tie. And he was, more unexpectedly, Godfrey Willis, program vice-president of IBC. They were, Janet thought, certainly scraping the top of the barrel.

"—Pulitzer Prize for national reporting when he was still in his middle twenties," Willis said, his voice grave, almost ponderous. "His reporting from Vietnam, first for the New York *Chronicle* and later for the magazine *Manhattan,* was widely acclaimed as the most accurate to come in those days from that troubled country. It was often in sharp contrast to the optimistic official reports emanating from American military sources during the Johnson Administration. At one time the Army threatened to withdraw his accreditation as a correspondent, but wiser heads prevailed. He came to the Independent Broadcasting Corporation as executive producer of news almost six years ago."

She was still standing in front of the big television set, looking down at it. Phil Whitmore came up and stood beside her. He had a glass in each hand and held one toward her, but she did not seem to see it. He stood with her and looked with her at the solemn face on the screen and listened to the heavily grave voice.

"Death is believed to have resulted from natural causes," Willis said. "But because of the unusual circumstances surrounding it, a police investigation may be instituted, according to Captain of Detectives John Stein, commanding the Homicide Squad, Manhattan North. The news we bring to you tonight is very sad news indeed to those of us here at IBC who have been his colleagues for so many—"

Phil Whitmore reached down and switched off the television set. A vertical white line crossed the screen and then the screen went dark. Janet did not move. She stood and looked at the blank screen and seemed yet to be listening to a stilled voice.

But she obeyed Phil Whitmore's hands and walked across the room and sat in the chair he guided her to. She even took the glass he reached out to her. But she took it automatically in her hand and merely held it. After a moment he took the glass from her and put it on a table. Finally she spoke.

"He seemed so well yesterday," Janet Osborne said. Her voice was uninflected. It was as if she were reading aloud from something not very interesting. "He seemed so strong."

"I'll call the office," Phil said. "See what the straight of it is."

She did not say anything, or look at him. He said, "Did you hear me, Jan?" and then she did look toward him. He thought there was blankness in her eyes.

She said, "Yes, I heard you."

He went to the telephone and dialed. He said, "City desk, please," and, after a moment, "Al? Phil Whitmore. About Clay Carter. Mind telling me what's come through on it?"

After that, Phil said nothing for some minutes. Then he said, "Yeah," and was silent again. Then he said, "Yes, Al. We were in Vietnam at the same time." He paused for a moment. He said, "It sure as hell is," and came back into the living room.

Janet had taken her glass from the table and, he thought, had drunk a little from it. When he stood in front of her and looked down at her she put the glass down again. She looked up at him. Her eyes, he thought, were not quite so blank. He moved a chair so he could sit on it facing her.

"Yes," he said. "It was Clay."

"Of course it was Clay. Tell me."

"A man who works for him found him," Whitmore told her. "A man named Johnson."

"Cyril Johnson," Janet said. "Clay mentioned him last night."

There was still no inflection in her voice. It was still as if she were reading words somebody else had written for her to read.

"Yes," Phil said. "Seems that around seven this

evening Clay had told this man Johnson to bring him out a drink. To the pool. In hot weather, seems Clay often had a swim around six in the evening. There's this pool back of the house. Wouldn't expect anybody to have a private swimming pool here in town, would you? Even such a hell of a way uptown. But Clay had."

"He told me about it. His grandfather had it put in years ago. Johnson took a drink out to him?"

"At seven sharp, Johnson says. Seems Clay was going out to dinner. Johnson says he doesn't know where, or with whom. Says Mr. Carter told him around six he wasn't eating at home after all. 'And I'd started dinner,' Johnson said. We've got a man up there. So—"

Cyril Johnson had carried a drink out to the pool at seven.

He had found Clayton Carter lying on his side by the edge of the pool. He was so close to the pool that one foot dangled into the water. A small portable television set was on the tiles near him. It was plugged into a socket a few feet away from the pool. It was set at Channel 4. It was turned on, but not operating.

Clayton Carter was wearing swimming trunks. Johnson had put the drink down on a table and said something. He thought he had said, "Here's your drink, sir." Something like that, anyway. He had got no answer. He had gone over to Carter and said, "Mr. Carter, sir," and then, more loudly, *Mr. Carter!*"

"What he says," Phil said. "He says, 'I thought maybe he was asleep. Only I knew he wasn't.' "

"He said that to the *Chronicle* man?"

"To everybody, apparently," Phil told her. "To Larry Knight, the *Chronicle* man. And to somebody from the *News*. And to the police, Jan."

He paused for a moment. She lifted her glass rather abruptly and drank from it. The blankness, he thought, had gone out of her eyes. She said, "The police?" The dullness had gone out of her voice.

"When he couldn't rouse Clay, Johnson called for an ambulance," Whitmore told her. "That brought a cruise car, of course."

"But," she said, "it was 'natural causes' on TV."

"What they thought at first, anyway. A heart attack, presumably. Only, his regular doctor wouldn't sign a certificate. And—well, they've taken Clay's body to the morgue, Jan. For an autopsy. And, temporarily anyway, it's listed as a suspicious death. Probably accidental, they think. They took the little TV down to the police lab."

She shook her head slowly.

"If the little TV he was using—"

"To monitor the NBC Sunday news," she said. "He called it the 'gimmick.' I don't think he'd had it very long."

"Whatever he was listening to. Looking at. It was turned on. But it was dead. As if it were shorted out. When—well, when he turned it on, he may have been sitting on the edge of the pool. With his feet in the water, maybe. Or—well, just wet all over. And if there was faulty insulation in the TV set . . ."

"But the set was almost new, I think."

"It could be," Philip Whitmore said, "that that's what made the police wonder, dear."

"I don't—" she said, but did not finish. She shook her head. She picked her glass up and drank from it, this time deeply. She put the glass down again. She looked toward him, but he did not think that, in any real sense, she saw him.

"There's not much of anything to say, is there?" Phil Whitmore said. "He was a hell of a good reporter. Which isn't anything to say."

Finally, she looked at him as if she saw him.

"Not now there isn't," she said. "It's—it's just stunning. He was laughing, yesterday. He was trying out a new serve. And he was a good reporter, wasn't he?"

"And a good guy," he said.

"And a good guy. We're not making much sense, are we?"

"There are times people don't, Jan. You're in what they call 'shock,' aren't you? It's—the thing is, dear, I'm sorry as hell."

"I'll be all right," Janet said. "Why don't you just go along home, Phil? I'll be all right."

He reached across the table and took her hand. It tightened in his, then relaxed. He released her hand and stood up. He said, "Good night, Janet," and walked to the door. He had his hand on the knob when she spoke.

"Good night, Phil," she said, and then she got up from her chair and walked toward him. Again she said, "Good night," and now her voice sounded, to both of them, like her voice again.

"Call me tomorrow sometime," she said. "Tomorrow evening. I may be late getting here. After nine, perhaps."

His hands moved a little, as if he were about to reach out to her. But he did not reach out to her.

"I'll call tomorrow," Phil said, and there seemed to be a kind of thickness in his voice. He went down the stairs. When she heard the vestibule door open and close behind him, Janet closed the door to her apartment and notched the chain on. Was it Clay who had made her promise to chain her door at night? No, it's Phil who's always made such a point of that.

5

ASSISTANT DISTRICT ATTORNEY Bernard Simmons, deputy chief, Homicide Bureau, office of the District Attorney, County and State of New York, got to his office at a little after nine Monday morning, more or less dragging his title behind him. He had got to bed at a little after three, following an interminable conference with an attorney whose client was to appear in court that morning—was, probably, waiting in court as Simmons sat down at his desk and ran a hand over the perspiring forehead of a somewhat aching head. He had planned a very different evening before the maître d' at Charles had told him there was a telephone call for him.

But when defense attorneys offer pleas, assistant district attorneys have to listen, particularly when arraignment is only a few hours away. Involuntary manslaughter? Come off it. Possibly voluntary manslaughter, then, although the client would of course have to be consulted. No. Possibly second degree. With a recommendation of leniency? Because the client was just a nutso kid, with no previous record. Well—

"You'll never get murder one. You won't even get them to indict for murder one."

Bernie had gone, step by step, over the evidence against Jones, black—actually, a rather light brown—who perhaps had merely meant to frighten an errant girl friend with his Saturday night special, who perhaps had thought the bullet from the little gun would go feet above her head. It had not.

"He's just a nutso kid, Mr. Simmons."

"A nutso kid with a crummy little gun. All right, she was a tramp. And he didn't know it until a few minutes before he began to wave the gun at her. And he maybe did think they were going to get married and get out of Harlem and go back South. Second degree, Mr. Zirkin, and we won't pressure the judge on the sentence. O.K.?"

It had been almost two-thirty when Arthur Zirkin had finally agreed it might be O.K., subject, of course, to the decision of his client.

Bernie Simmons considered an aspirin and reached toward his In basket. The telephone bell rang. Damn Alexander Graham Bell, as Nora had suggested. "Simmons" into the telephone. Then he said, "All right, Mary," to Mary Leffing, who was his secretary when the chief of the Homicide Bureau didn't need her. "I'll get along."

He went up one floor by elevator. Brian Hagerty's secretary told him to go right along in.

Brian Hagerty's office was fairly large and comfortably cool. Hagerty's desk was clear except for a sheaf of papers in front of the District Attorney, County of New York. The office of New York County District Attorney is an elective one. For a good many years, while political squabbles in the city went on incessantly, nobody had nominated anyone but Brian Hagerty for District Attorney.

"Morning, Simmons," Hagerty said. "You look as if you had a bad night. Sit down."

"A long night, anyway," Bernie said, and sat down. "Zirkin wants to cop a plea for a kid who killed his girl friend. The kid's girl friend, not Zirkin's."

"You're muzzy this morning. Don't blame you. Zirkin leaves me muzzy, too. So?"

"Second degree. No opposition to a plea for leniency. I had Randolph go along for us. O.K., sir?"

"Your case, Counselor. I suppose our learned friend started with discharge of a firearm in a populated area?"

"Involuntary manslaughter," Bernie said.

"Zirkin's losing his grip," District Attorney Hagerty said. "You've heard about Clayton Carter?"

"Carter? I know who he is, of course."

"Was," Hagerty said. "Don't you read the papers, Simmons? Listen to the radio?"

"Chief," Bernie said, "I finally got to bed at three o'clock this morning. Fell all over myself getting here at all. The hacker was listening to the hit parade, not the news. I told him to turn the damn thing off."

"Clayton Carter was found dead beside his swimming pool about seven last night," Hagerty said. "Apparently, he'd been sitting on the edge of the pool. He was alone there, so Homicide North is guessing what happened. The guess is, he reached over to turn the TV on and was electrocuted."

Bernie Simmons said he'd be damned. Hagerty waited to be told why.

"He was using that little TV set of his Saturday," Bernie said. "Up in the country at some people's named

Streeter. Using it by their pool. It was working all right then. If it's the same set, of course."

Briefly, he told Hagerty about the afternoon and evening at Agnes and Paul Streeter's. Yes, he had known the Streeters for some time. No, he had never met Clayton Carter before; had seen him, of course, on television. Carter had had a girl with him. A Janet Osborne. "She's his assistant at IBC."

"And Miss Curran was with you, I suppose?"

There are a good many people connected with the office of the District Attorney, County of New York. Things get around among them.

"Yes, I took Nora up. For tennis. To get out of this damn mugginess."

"And met Carter the day before he died," Hagerty said. "And his TV set was working all right?"

"Seemed to be. Oh, the battery ran down. He had to plug it in for a recharge."

"And Carter himself?"

Bernie raised his very red eyebrows.

"Seem all right to you? Cheerful? That sort of thing?"

"To me. I'd never met him before, Chief."

"Getting along all right with this girl he brought along? Close, they seem to you?"

"I guess so, I wasn't—well, paying a lot of attention to them, I suppose. Not knowing he was going to be— call it a case for Johnny Stein."

"And so for us," Hagerty said. "For you, Bernard."

Hagerty seldom used their first names to members of his staff. He never used diminutives.

"Didn't seem depressed, I gather," Hagerty said. "Like, say, a man who was thinking of killing himself?"

"Not to me. He was a little annoyed by the man who was doing the Saturday night news show. Overheard him talking to Miss Osborne about him. Killing himself, sir?"

"A quick way," Hagerty said. "Reasonably painless, probably. Theory of the electric chair, anyway. Quick, efficient. Doesn't get blood all over the place. No strain on the witnesses. Who don't have to throw the switch, of course. You ever get fed up with these law-and-order bastards, Bernard?"

"Well," Bernie said, "we're law and order, Chief. Part of it, anyway."

"Not that part," Hagerty said. "Here." He pushed the sheaf of paper across his desk to Bernie Simmons.

"Lab report on the TV set," Hagerty said. "Autopsy report on Carter. Full cooperation with the police, of course." He flicked the intercom. "Miss Parsons, you can send Wallings in when Mr. Simmons leaves."

Bernie Simmons left. He took the sheaf of papers with him.

Clayton Carter had been a Caucasian male, an even six feet tall. He had weighed a hundred and sixty-three pounds. He had been in his early-to-mid forties. There had been no organic impairment which would account for sudden death. There was evidence of muscular tetanic spasm and slight edema of the lungs. On the thumb and forefinger of the right hand there were small burns, probably electrical. (Microscopic examination of tissues not yet completed.) Presumed cause of death: electrocution by standard household current.

The television set was of German manufacture. The model had been on the market for less than a year. In addition to TV signals, it could receive AM and FM radio.

Subject set was defective in that insulation was worn, or scraped, away on the main intake wire at a point where it touched the metal casing of the set. Anyone touching the set while it was plugged in to a 115-volt socket would experience a severe shock. If such a person were grounded—had his feet in water, for example—the shock might well be lethal.

The set had a serial number, which was given. The appliance shop from which it had been purchased probably could be traced through the number. Except for the faulty insulation, the set was in good condition. It seemed to be relatively new. The date of its manufacture could probably, by means of the serial number, be obtained from the manufacturer in West Germany.

A miniature TV set, all right Saturday evening, lethal twenty-four hours later. A Caucasian male, with an effective service Saturday afternoon and good ground strokes, Sunday night on an autopsy table. A wire carrying 115 volts, with insulation worn—or scraped—away. Feet dangling in the water of a swimming pool. Who the hell had a private swimming pool in Manhattan—even (Bernie looked again at the autopsy report) somewhere in the upper Nineties on Riverside Drive? Who would know enough about the insides of a TV set to scrape insulation from the right wire? Not ADA Bernard Simmons, certainly. But Bernard Simmons would help to find out. Not do the work of the police for them, of course. Only to evaluate the evidence when they had collected it and authorize whatever charge it warranted.

Bernie flicked his intercom. He got from it, "Yes, Mr. Simmons?" Of course, Mary Leffing could rustle up some coffee. She'd be glad to. "Just a—one moment, Mr. Simmons." Off mike, "Mr. Simmons's office." Pause. "Yes, he is, Captain. Just a moment, please."

Mary Leffing came back on the intercom. She said,

"Captain Stein for you. I'll bring the coffee."

Bernie Simmons had already picked up the telephone. He said, "Morning, Johnny."

"We're crawling with reporters," Detective Captain John Stein, commanding Homicide, Manhattan North, told him. "On the Carter kill. I gather you're going to sit in. Want to come up and start now? Guide our faltering footsteps, Counselor?"

John Stein sounded grumpy. He calls Simmons "Counselor" only when he is grumpy. "As usual," he added.

Simmons said, "Kill, Johnny?"

"From the lab's report on the TV set, kill. You haven't got to that yet?"

"Worn or scraped, it says," Bernie told him.

"You're behind us," Stein said. "Microscope shows scraped, Sergeant Gratzioni says. Possibly with a pocketknife. Nick in the knife blade. Maybe the lab could identify the knife if we turn it up. Might do a match with the scorings on the wire, Gratzioni thinks. No suitable knife in Carter's effects. Or that they can find in this house of his. If you were thinking he did it himself, Bernie?"

Mary Leffing came in with a pot of coffee—a pot, no less. Bernie said, "Thanks, dear," and Stein said, "What the hell, Counselor?"

Bernie's lips formed the first smile of the morning. He said, "Not you, Captain dear. Mary, for coffee. You at your office, John?"

At the moment, Captain John Stein was in his office off the squad room of Homicide, Manhattan North. Men from the precinct were up on Riverside Drive. But with this supplement to the lab report, Stein was going up to Carter's house and taking Paul Lane with him.

"And," Stein said, "I suppose you want to sit in, Bernie."

"If I won't be in the way," Bernie Simmons said, making his voice meek enough to get a short laugh from Stein. "What the chief wants," Bernie added.

Stein said, "See you," and hung up.

Bernie drank coffee, which was still warm enough. Everything was warm enough on this July day. He smoked a cigarette with the coffee. He told Mary Leffing where he would be and that Homicide North could reach him if a roof fell in. He went down to a stifling sidewalk and thought of a cab and decided on the subway. The air in the subway car to Grand Central hadn't been changed in a generation. Neither had the air in the shuttle car, nor the air in the Broadway–Seventh Avenue express. It was just as muggily hot when he climbed to the surface at Ninety-sixth Street. Then a miracle intervened. The cab was air-conditioned. The last fare had been a cigar smoker, but one can't have everything. New Yorkers learn not to look even the most trivial of miracles in the teeth.

Clayton Carter's narrow house surprised Bernard Simmons as, some thirty-six hours before, it had surprised Janet Osborne. Now there were two cruise cars parked in front of it and two unmarked sedans. One would have brought men from the precinct squad; the other Captain John Stein and Detective (1st gr.) Paul Lane. On the other side of the street there was a truck with INDEPENDENT BROADCASTING CORPORATION lettered on it. A uniformed patrolman was standing in front of the door of the narrow house. He said, "No press, mister," as Simmons crossed the sidewalk toward him.

Bernie said he wasn't press and showed an ID card to prove it.

It was cool in the house when Bernie went into

it. Stein and Paul Lane were in a narrow living room, sitting in deep chairs. A man with pale brown skin was sitting on the edge of a chair less deep. He wore a white jacket and a white shirt and a black necktie. He stood up as Bernie went into the room.

Stein said, "Hi, Counselor." He said, "This is Cyril Johnson. This is Assistant District Attorney Simmons, Mr. Johnson."

Johnson said, "Sir," and Bernie said, "Good morning, Mr. Johnson."

"Mr. Johnson found his employer's body last night," Stein said. "He was just starting to tell us about it. Sit down, won't you, and tell us about it."

Johnson sat down, again on the edge of his chair.

"Most Sunday evenings in the summer," Johnson said, "he went to the pool for a dip before dinner." His accent was British. Up from Jamaica, Bernie thought.

"At seven, after the six-thirty news, I took a drink out to him. That was the schedule." (The word was "shedule" on Johnson's lips.) "Usually I then prepared his dinner, but last night he had planned to dine out. He had told me that before he went out to the pool."

"You had expected him to have dinner here?"

"Yes, sir. I had a joint in the oven, sir."

"Go on. You took the drink out to him." That was Stein.

"Yes, sir. A gin and tonic."

"Yes. And?"

"He was lying on his side by the pool. His left side, sir. Quite close to the pool. It was sunny where he was lying. At first I thought—I suppose I thought that he was just resting in the sun. Only, I suppose I didn't really, sir. He—I mean it just didn't look like that, sir."

Johnson had said something. He didn't remember what. He had put the drink down on a table and squatted down by Carter and spoken again. "I said, 'Mr. *Carter*, sir.'" Unanswered, he had touched Carter's shoulder. "In case he was asleep." The body—he knew then that it was a body, no longer a man—had moved a little at his touch, had started to roll toward the pool. He had gone into the house and called Carter's doctor. Then, on the doctor's advice, he had called for an ambulance. The doctor, who lived nearby, had got there first. Clayton Carter had been dead when he got there. He had, the physician thought, been dead for not more than an hour. The doctor assumed a heart attack.

"He didn't sound sure about it, sir. Seemed sort of puzzled."

"We've been in touch with the doctor, Bernie," Stein said. "He'd given Carter an annual checkup a couple of months ago. Hadn't found anything wrong with his heart. Nothing much else wrong with him. Told him he smoked too much."

Reminded, Bernie Simmons lighted a cigarette. "This portable television set of his," Bernie said. "Where was it, Mr. Johnson?"

It had been on the tiles, near the edge of the pool. Yes, it had been within reach of Carter when, and if, Carter had been sitting on the edge of the pool. Yes, it had been plugged into an electric socket. No, neither picture nor sound had been coming from the set when Johnson had carried the gin and tonic out to the pool.

"Tuned to Channel Four, Bernie," Stein said. "According to the boys in the cruise car. One of the patrolmen started to pick it up to get it out of the way, but his sidekick said they'd better unplug it first. Saved the force a patrolman, maybe. Or just saved a patrolman a nasty shock, since he wasn't wet. The way Carter was."

"This set," Bernie said. "Happen to know how long he'd had it, Mr. Johnson?"

Johnson thought only a few months. He did not know exactly.

"Took it around with him a good deal?"

"Pretty much always, I think, sir. Of course, when he was at home, he used that one over there." He pointed to a big television set against a wall of the long narrow room. The screen of the set stared at them blankly.

"There's another set in his bedroom," Johnson said. "Where he could see it from his bed. And there's one in my quarters, sir. On the top floor."

"This little set," Bernie said. "Did he ever tinker with it, that you know of? I mean, open it up. If, say, it got out of whack?"

"Sir?"

"Didn't work properly," Bernie said. "Needed repair. Adjustment. That sort of thing."

Johnson had never seen his employer do anything to the portable set. Except, of course, plug it in when the battery needed recharging.

"Mr. Johnson, you and Mr. Carter were the only people living here in the house?" Stein said.

"Just the two of us, sir. Oh, when we gave a big party, Mr. Carter had an agency send people in, of course. The rest of the time, I did for him, sir."

"There isn't any Mrs. Carter, I take it," Stein said.

For the first time, the brown-faced man hesitated. He covered hesitation with a somewhat drawn-out "Well." They waited.

"Not in my time, sir," Johnson said. "That would be two years ago last month. But I believe there was a Mrs. Carter some time ago. She doesn't live here now. When he was showing me around the house, Mr. Carter showed me a door and said something about its leading to what used to be his wife's room. We didn't go in, sir. He just said it was a room I wouldn't have to bother with. Or have the cleaning woman bother with. There's a cleaning woman comes in four days a week. She doesn't live in."

"He just said his wife doesn't live here now," Bernie said. "Did you gather that she does live somewhere, Mr. Johnson? From the way he spoke about her? I mean, not as if she were dead?"

"I don't really know, sir. He never spoke about her to me. But I had a feeling she had left him. Not that she'd died."

"He never mentioned her? Didn't even mention her name?"

"No, sir. After all, I'm—I was—his servant, sir."

Bernie half expected Cyril Johnson to point out that he knew his place. Johnson did not.

"Something I do re—" Johnson said and was interrupted by a wail. To Bernie Simmons it sounded rather like the cry of a very mournful baby. It was accompanied by a soft, spaced thudding. The sounds seemed to come through the door which opened from the narrow living room into the entrance hall. A long, sleek cat with pointed dark brown ears and a brown mask appeared in the doorway. He said "Yowowowah," holding it. He repeated the same sound. He did not come into the room.

"It's out there, Mao," Johnson said. "I put it down for you."

Mao repeated what he had said before. He stared at Cyril Johnson through large, very blue eyes.

"He won't eat," Johnson said. "He won't eat a thing. Every morning at around eight he goes up to the door to Mr. Carter's bedroom and makes those noises he makes and Mr. Carter lets him in. He only stays a few minutes and then he comes down to the kitchen and I give him his breakfast. This morning, of course, the bedroom door was open and—and—"

"Mr. Carter wasn't there," Bernie said. "We know, Mao."

The long Siamese repeated what he had said before, his tone even more disconsolate. He turned, and they heard him softly padding upstairs.

"Gone back to look again," Johnson said. "He just can't believe it."

"They don't care about people," Paul Lane said. "Just about places."

Bernie looked at him.

"Well," Lane said, "that's what everybody says, anyway."

"Everybody is an ass, Paul," Bernie said. "As was once said about the law. Mao probably will go on looking for days. In the same places, time after time. Oh, he'll give up, finally. Like anybody else does. You were about to remember something, Mr. Johnson?"

"About a year ago," Johnson said. "I think it was on a Sunday. Yes, I remember. It was raining, so I brought Mr. Carter's drink in here. I heard the telephone ringing on my way in, but when I got here, he'd already answered it. I couldn't help overhearing, sir."

"What did you hear?"

"Mr. Carter said, 'Grace doesn't live here any more. Hadn't you heard?' Then he hung up."

"You're sure he said 'any more'?" Simmons asked.

That was the way Johnson remembered it.

"You think Mr. Carter may have been talking about his wife?"

"I'm sure I don't know, sir. You were asking about

Mrs. Carter. It was just something I remembered."

Bernie looked at John Stein and raised his red eyebrows.

"You may as well show us where you found Mr. Carter last night," Stein said.

They followed Johnson the length of the long narrow room and into the back end of the hall, then through a narrow and immaculate kitchen and through a room beyond it, with a bar along one wall. The house made up in depth what it lacked in width. Johnson opened another door, and they went out onto a narrow flagged terrace, with terrace furniture on it. It was a little like the Streeters' country terrace, Bernie thought, only much smaller.

The pool, too, was smaller. They stepped from the terrace to the tiling which surrounded the pool. The pool occupied most of the yard behind the house. To the right, it reached beyond the house toward a tall apartment building. A tall green fence of narrow boards surrounded the yard. Sunlight sifted through the fence but did not reach as far as the pool.

Johnson led them to the right for a dozen feet or so and said, "About here he was lying, close to the edge. I put his drink down there." He pointed to a white metal table.

"The TV set?"

"About there, sir."

He indicated a place some three feet from the spot he had said Clayton Carter's body had lain.

"And there's where he had it plugged in."

He pointed to the closed outdoor cap of an electric socket. It was very close to the edge of the pool.

"Supposed to be ten feet from the pool," Lane said. "There's a law about it."

Nobody responded.

There was nothing for them there. There was only shining pale-green tile around a swimming pool; only streaks of sunlight on grass which had the tired look of city grass.

"They take pictures?" Bernie asked.

John Stein shook his head. "Still looked like heart attack," he said. "Listed suspicious after they got the body to Bellevue. Carter's doctor said he couldn't sign a certificate."

They went back into the house. They went up the staircase to the second floor. At the head of the stairs, a door stood open. "Yes," Johnson said, "Mr. Carter's room." They went into the room, which was as narrow as the living room below it, but not so long.

At the back end of the room there was a three-quarters bed against the wall. The bed was neatly made up and Mao was crouched on it, his chin on his forepaws. He raised his head abruptly when Stein led the way into the room. Then he yowled. The yowl ended in something like a snarl.

"Wrong people," Bernie said, and Mao flowed to his four feet and leaped from the bed. He slid at a trot between intervening legs, and they heard him thumping down the stairs.

There was a closed door at either end of the bed against the back wall of Carter's room. Under a wide window on the front—a window almost the full width of the room—there was a big desk facing the room, with a typewriter on a stand at right angles to it. A floor lamp stood so it would throw light on both desk and typewriter.

"He worked here sometimes," Johnson said. "Sometimes I'd hear his typewriter. On Saturdays and Sundays, mostly. Sometimes at night."

Midway of the room there were two chairs, with a table between them. They faced toward a big television set. There was a large ashtray, immaculately clean, on the table.

There was nothing on the top of the desk except another ashtray, a calendar pad and a white telephone.

"You straightened up this room when, Mr. Johnson?" Bernie said.

"Early this morning," Johnson said. "Before the other policemen came. I hope that was all right, sir. Just emptied the ashtrays and brushed up a little, sir."

"It was quite all right," Bernie said. "The bed was made up the way it is now, I suppose? Hadn't been slept in."

"Oh, no, sir. Mr. Carter was—"

"I know. Some people take afternoon naps, of course. Mr. Carter was up here yesterday afternoon, I suppose?"

"Yes, sir. There were cigarette ends in both ashtrays. And he was up here to change to go to the pool, of course."

John Stein had gone over to the chair behind the desk. He spoke from there. "These other policemen," he said. "I suppose they went through this desk?"

"They asked me if Mr. Carter had a pocketknife, sir. I told them I'd never seen him use one. They said they'd look around and came up here. I don't know whether they looked through the desk, sir. They did look at all the kitchen knives."

Stein said, "Mmmm," and took a leather-bound black book out of the desk's center drawer. He began to flick through it, using the lettered tabs. He turned several pages and looked across the desk at Bernie Simmons and nodded his head.

"Yes," he said. "Under G. Just 'Grace.' Address' in the East Seventies. Could be the Grace who doesn't live here any more."

He opened a deep bottom drawer of the desk and found a Manhattan telephone directory and flicked through it. He stopped a page with a finger. "Carter, Mrs. Grace," he said. "Right address." He noted down the address and telephone number on a memo pad he found in the top drawer.

Bernie walked around behind the desk beside Captain John Stein. They both looked at the calendar pad.

The sheet for the day before, Sunday, was uppermost. Nothing was written on it. The sheet for Monday had "Ck. L. Con." on it, which didn't, at the moment, mean anything. On the sheet for the previous Saturday was "Str. 3:30. Take J. and gear."

That was clear enough to Bernie, and he explained it to Stein, who said, "Keeping things to yourself, Counselor?"

"Nothing significant," Bernie said. "Carter had a pretty good first service. Janet Osborne's very good-looking. Works with him at the network. Did until last night, anyway. Used to work for the Bartwell Industries, she told Nora. Plays a nice game of tennis."

"She and Carter?"

Bernie said he wouldn't know. He hadn't seen enough of them even to guess.

They came from behind the desk and walked to the back of the room together. Stein said, "Closet?" and pointed at the door at the head of the made-up bed. Johnson went to the door and opened it and switched on a light in the walk-in closet.

Carter had had a good many clothes. Suits and odd jackets were on hangers on either side of the deep closet. At the end of it was a chest of drawers, with a mirror above it. An electric razor in its case was on top of the chest. A wire ran down from the case to an electric socket. The razor case did not close tightly, and a small light showed through the crack. Bernie opened the case and pulled the cord out of the charging shaver.

"No," Stein said, "he won't be shaving any more. The men who were here earlier, Mr. Johnson. They go through the clothes looking for a knife? Anything like that?"

"Yes, sir. I hung Mr. Carter's things back up after they'd finished. I hope that was all right, sir?"

Stein said it had been quite all right. They went out of the closet and around the bed to the other door. "To the bathroom," Johnson said, and opened the door.

It opened on a corridor across the house from the main hall. There was another closed door at the far end of the corridor. The bathroom door on the side of the corridor was open.

The bathroom was large and very modern. It was done in blue tile; the tub, with sliding glass panels—open—matched the tile. There were thick white bath towels on racks. None of them appeared to have been used. "Mr. Carter didn't like to use a towel twice," Johnson said. "He always showered before he went into the pool, sir. I brought up a fresh towel last night before I made his drink."

There was nothing for them in the bathroom, as there had been nothing at the pool. They went back into the corridor. The door at the end of it was locked.

"Door to the other bedroom," Johnson said. "The one he told me not to bother with."

"You have a key to it?"

"Not to this one, no. I've got one probably fits

the other door—the one in the main hall. You want to get into the room, sir?"

They did.

Johnson went out through Carter's bedroom into the hall and, after a moment, they could hear a key in a rather distant lock. It worked and they could hear Johnson coming toward them through the other room. His footfalls were muffled, apparently on carpeting. He opened the door and they went into the bedroom which adjoined Clayton Carter's.

In shape and dimension it was almost identical with the room which had been Carter's. Yet it was quite different. The floor was covered with pale yellow carpet. There was a large window, draped by curtains of a deeper yellow at the end of the room. In the inner wall there was a fireplace, with logs arranged symmetrically in it. Bernie had a feeling that they were show logs, meant to dress a fireplace, not to be burned.

The big bed—probably what they call king-size, Bernie Simmons thought—was opposite the fireplace, its headboard against the wall. It was smoothly covered with a white spread. Under the window at the end of the room there was a dressing table, with a mirror over it and the sheath of a fluorescent tube above the mirror.

Above the head of the big bed there was a tall crucifix, the frame of which appeared to have been permanently secured to the wall.

"Was Mr. Carter a Roman Catholic, do you know?" Bernie asked Johnson. As a nominal Episcopalian, Bernie was careful to stress the "Roman."

Johnson didn't know. The subject had not come up. "I'm chapel, myself," Johnson added.

The closet of this room was like that in the other room. But there was nothing in it. The drawers of the dressing table were empty. No, Bernie found, not entirely empty. In a corner of the shallow central drawer, there was a single bobby pin. It was pale gold in color. He held it out to John Stein.

"When you go to see Mrs. Carter," Bernie said, "you'll probably find a blonde."

Stein agreed he'd probably find a blonde.

"And," Bernie said, "a Roman Catholic, don't you think, Johnny?"

Stein thought it seemed likely.

"They're generally pretty strict about divorce," Bernie said.

Stein said he'd heard they were.

"Not," Bernie said, "that I use 'they' in any pejorative sense."

"It takes all kinds, Bernie," Stein said.

6

GRACE CARTER WAS BLOND, as Bernie Simmons had deduced from a bobby pin. She was also beautiful. When she came down a spiral staircase from the second floor of the duplex in the East Seventies, she came down it with grace and dignity, both difficult to attain on a spiral staircase.

She had made no objection to seeing Captain John Stein of the New York Police Department. A maid in a green uniform had opened the door on the first floor of a four-story brick house. Stein had expected a tall apartment building and had been slightly surprised to find the address he had written down turned out to be that of a town house which, by comparison with its neighbors, looked as if it might have stood there almost forever.

The maid thought Mrs. Carter was in. If Captain —Stein, was it?—would wait a moment, she would tell Mrs. Carter he was there. The maid, who was thin to the point of being stringy, was very grave, as, Stein assumed, befitted a servant in a house of mourning. She closed the door, with Stein outside it. But it was less than a minute before she opened the door again and said that if the captain would come in, Mrs. Carter would be right down.

Coming down the spiral staircase, Grace Carter wore a dark green housecoat, which fitted with the utmost smoothness a body well worth fitting. Her blond hair waved down to her shoulders. Her blue eyes were wide-set; her mouth was perhaps a little small. She did not look as if she had been crying, but the smile on her lips was a small, tight smile.

Stein was sorry to bother her at such a time. He was one of those investigating Mr. Carter's sudden death. It was a matter of routine. He would try to make it as brief as possible.

"Sudden death?" Grace said. "According to the television news, somebody killed him. That's why you're here, isn't it?"

She had a light, clear voice. It was not an emotional voice; Stein could hear no strain in it.

"I'm afraid that's the way it looks," John Stein said. "I thought you might be able—"

Mrs. Carter did not wait to hear what Stein thought she might be able to do. She raised her voice a little and said, "Irene?"

The maid in the green uniform came through a door behind the staircase, which spiraled down in a corner of the big, almost square room. She said, "Yes, Mrs. Carter?"

"Will you bring us some coffee?" Grace Carter said. "I'm sure the captain would like some coffee."

Irene said, "Yes, Mrs. Carter," and went back

through the doorway under the staircase. Grace Carter said they might as well sit down, and went to a chair in front of a blond mahogany coffee table and sat in it. Stein went to a chair which, diagonally, faced hers.

"It is Stein, isn't it?" Grace Carter said. "I think that's what Irene said. Captain Stein?"

"Yes, Mrs. Carter. John Stein. I'm a homicide detective."

"And you think there may be some way I can help you," she said. "I don't know how, but of course I will if I can. Poor dear Clay. Only, we've been separated for two years, you see, so I don't see how I—"

The maid came in with a silver tray with a silver coffeepot on it, and cream and sugar in silver receptacles which, in design, matched the pot. There were also rather fragile-looking white cups on the tray. Irene put the tray down on the coffee table and said, "Will there be anything more, Mrs. Carter?"

"Not unless the captain—?"

Stein said that coffee would be fine, and that it was very kind of Mrs. Carter. He also said, "Thank you, Irene." Irene made an accepting sound, and went away. Grace Carter poured coffee into fragile cups. Stein had his black. It was very good coffee.

"In cases like this," Stein said, "we try to find out what we can about—well, about the"—he paused to light the cigarette Grace Carter had between her deftly colored lips—"victim," he said, and lighted a cigarette of his own.

"Poor dear Clay," she said. "I can't really believe it. That he'd ever be a *victim*. I mean, it just—oh, it just seems all wrong."

There didn't seem to be any responsive answer to that—except that murder is always wrong. Stein made an "Mmmm" sound, to show he had heard her. He sipped from his cup. She looked at him with what he took to be expectancy in her blue eyes.

"Anything you can tell me about him," Stein said.

"I don't know," Grace Carter said. "Oh, he had a lot of money. The Carters have always had, of course. He didn't have to work the way he did. Go to those awful places and write about them. We could have gone to lovely places. Gone together. Paris. Venice. Would you believe I've never been in Venice? And lived here, instead of in that weird place on Riverside. Nobody lives on Riverside Drive nowadays."

There seemed to be no point in questioning her rather abrupt dismissal of Riverside Drive. Stein said, "A lot of money, Mrs. Carter?"

"Oodles," she said, unexpectedly to Stein's ears. "The Carters have always had. And instead of living as we should have, Clay spent years in Vietnam. Writing what a lot of people think were unpatriotic articles about what our country was doing there. And then putting all that money into this network which says such unpleasant things about our President. Scurrilous things, a lot of my friends think. And then just broadcasting for a company he owned all that stock in. Can you imagine?"

Stein saw no point in telling this brittle, obviously resentful woman that he could, without too much difficulty, imagine a man doing work which interested him. Even if he didn't have to.

"You said you and Mr. Carter could have lived here, Mrs. Carter. You mean here, in this building?"

"Of course. Clay owned it. Inherited it from his father. The two top floors are rented now, but we could have had the whole house, instead of that awful place on Riverside, where only—"

She looked at Stein's dark, handsome face and

stopped the sentence. Stein thought of several things to say and said none of them. He said, "You came to live here after you left Mr. Carter?"

"Yes. Clay arranged it. I'll say that for him."

"And I suppose this house will be yours now," Stein said. "And probably the rest of his estate. I'm assuming you and Mr. Carter were merely separated, not divorced?"

"God has set his hand against divorce," she said.

Stein said, "Oh," and managed to keep any inflection of query out of his voice. He hadn't heard from God recently, at least on that subject.

"You're not of my faith," Mrs. Carter told him. "His Holiness has made the divine meaning clear. If Clay and I had been divorced I could never have married again. I'd have been excommunicated. Denied the Holy Sacrament."

Stein said he saw.

"As for my inheriting Clay's estate," she said, "my lawyer says I'll have to get at least part of it. He says that's the law. Whatever his will says."

Detective (1st gr.) Paul Lane was, at the moment, trying to find out what Clayton Carter's will said. The address and telephone number of a law firm had turned up in Carter's address book. Of course, Lane might merely be sitting in a law firm's waiting room. Conceivably, the waiting room of the wrong law firm. Possibly to no avail in any case. Lawyers can be sticky people, thought Stein, who had passed his own bar examination a couple of years before.

"Yes, Mrs. Carter," Stein said. "You have what are called dower rights. Whatever your husband stipulated in his will. This is probably an impertinent question under the circumstances. An irrelevant one. You don't need to answer, of course. Do you plan—"

He did not finish, because Grace Carter obviously was not listening. She was looking away from him, toward the door between the big living room and the small entrance hall. The maid had closed it behind them when she showed him in.

It was open now. A man of medium height and breadth was standing in the doorway. He had slightly long, rather yellowish hair and a square face. He said, "Morning, d—" and broke the word in two. When he saw me, John Stein thought. And I didn't hear the doorbell ring, or see the maid go to answer the door. Of course, there may be another way to the front door from wherever Irene keeps herself.

"Why, Mr. Willis," Grace Carter said, and now her clear voice was deeper, a little husky. As would, Stein thought, be appropriate in the voice of the newly bereaved. "So good of you to come. I do appreciate it. This is Captain Stein, Mr. Willis. He's from the police."

"I just wanted to see whether there is anything we can do," Willis said. "All of us at the office. It's a terrible shock to all of us. And we know how you must be feeling. A police captain, you say? You don't waste much time, do you?"

"We try not to, Mr. Willis," Stein said and stood up. "John Stein. Homicide."

"Godfrey Willis," the square man said. "I'm with the network, IBC. As poor Carter was. A dreadful thing. Dreadful. You said 'homicide,' Captain? You mean, somebody *killed* Clay Carter?"

"It's listed as a suspicious death," Stein said. "The sort of thing we get called in on, sir. Along with a lot of other policemen, of course. We have to disturb a good many people, I'm afraid. Like Mrs. Carter here."

"But I *want* to do anything I can," Grace Carter said. "Help any way I can."

"We all do," Willis said. "Everybody who knew Carter will want to help in any way we can. Especially those of us who worked with him."

Stein was sure everybody would. He said that Mrs. Carter had already been very helpful. He looked at her as he said this and wondered if the expression on her face was, as it appeared to be, one of considerable surprise. He told her how much he appreciated her help, rubbing it in a little, and how much he regretted having had to bother her. "At such a time."

Still standing, even moving a little toward the door, Stein told Godfrey Willis that he hoped the policemen who were at the IBC offices weren't being too much of a bother. "We have to get the setup. Get the background."

Willis said he was sure everybody at IBC would want to do everything possible. He said, "We haven't any secrets, Captain."

Stein said he was sure they hadn't. "By the way," he said, "I'm not sure what Mr. Carter's precise position was at the network. I know he read the news, of course."

"And wrote most of it," Willis said. "Decided what we'd play up. Where we'd put the emphasis, if you follow me. Technically, he was executive producer of IBC news. Radio and television both, of course."

"And you, Mr. Willis? What is your capacity at the network? Just to get things straight in my mind."

"Vice-president in charge of programming," Willis said. "For the moment, until we get things straightened out, I'll have to take over the news department. I don't mean what you call read the news. A correspondent named Latham will do that. For now, anyway."

"As the man in charge of programs," Stein said, "I take it you're in overall charge of the news programs? That Mr. Carter was—how shall I put it?—under your direction?"

Willis said, "We—ll," drawing it out. For a moment, he did not go on. Then he said, "Technically, I suppose so. But Carter handled the news pretty much as he wanted to." He smiled slightly. "After all," he said, "one doesn't give orders to a director of the corporation, Captain."

"Mr. Carter was? A director, I mean?"

Clayton Carter had, assuredly, been on the board of directors of the Independent Broadcasting Company.

Stein once again thanked them both for their cooperation. He hoped he would not have to bother them too much in the future. He went through the entrance hall and out the front door of Mrs. Grace Carter's duplex apartment.

When he closed the door behind him, he tried to turn the outside knob. It did not turn. John Stein had assumed a snap lock, but one has to make sure about things.

The car was parked on the side of the street where no parking was allowed before 6 P.M. But the waiting driver was a patrolman in uniform, which made the necessary difference.

Of course, Stein thought, as they inched back to the headquarters of Homicide, Manhattan North, I may not have heard the doorbell. There are two doorways in the entrance hall, one into the living room and the other opening on I don't know what. A hallway, probably, leading back to other rooms. Irene may, obviously, have gone through that hall to answer the doorbell she heard and I didn't. Quite possibly, she let Mr. Willis in. I've no real evidence he had a key.

And the "d"-sound he made before he saw me doesn't prove anything. He might have been going to say, "Morning, dear," or even, "Morning, darling," before he saw Mrs. Carter had somebody he didn't know with her. And before Grace Carter cued him with her surprised "Why, Mr. Willis!" If she did cue him to formality. And a good many people use "dear" and even "darling" rather offhandedly to almost anybody. Mrs. Carter seems to me like one who might.

I never got around to asking her if she has plans to remarry. If she's as devoutly Catholic as she indicates, she couldn't before. Without being excommunicated, that is. Death has a finality denied divorce.

I wonder if Paul Lane got anything out of Carter's lawyer about the will. I wonder if Carter was as rich as his widow says he was. He owned stock in IBC, evidently. He was a director of the corporation, unless this Willis is lying. I don't suppose he is. About that, anyway.

"All right, Tom," Stein said as he got out of the car with its very long radio antenna. "Probably need you again. I'll call down if I do."

Tom said, "O.K., Captain," and Stein went upstairs.

Paul Lane was at his desk in the squad room. He nodded his head in response to Stein's beckoning gesture and followed him down the corridor to the office of Commander, Homicide Squad, Manhattan North.

* * * * *

It was about ten-thirty when Bernard Simmons found "Independent Broadcasting Company" on the directory board of an office building in Madison Ave-

nue. He found an elevator marked: "Express. 18–21."
There were a good many elevators, but only two so
marked. There were several people in the elevator
Bernie got into. Somebody had already pressed the
button numbered 18. It glowed red.

The elevator took off, very fast. Modern elevators
are needlessly in a hurry. Time isn't really all that
vital, Bernie thought. Except, perhaps, for those going
down in the evening after an office day.

The indicator showed 18, and Bernie got out into
a small room. He faced a desk with a sign saying "Information" and two telephones on it. Behind the desk
was a lacquered young woman, and on the wall behind
her INDEPENDENT BROADCASTING COMPANY
in commanding letters.

She could indeed help him. He would like to see
Miss Janet Osborne, if she was available.

"News Department. Nineteenth floor." He could
take that elevator, if he would. The nineteenth floor
would know whether Miss Osborne was available. The
eighteenth floor examined her fingernails, rather as if
she were seeing them for the first time.

The nineteenth floor was as lacquered as the one
below. It would see if Miss Osborne was free and whom
should she say was calling? Bernie noted the "whom"
and gave his name with its prefix. The nineteenth floor
said, "Oh, about *that*," and used one of the telephones,
after punching a button in its base. "He says he's a
district attorney," she told the telephone. "Named
Simon."

Which might, Bernie thought, be close enough.

"Through that way"—pointing—"and somebody
will show you her office."

Bernie went that way, which was marked: "News

Department. Studios A and B." Just beyond the door there was a small desk and a boy of fifteen or so with smooth long hair. "Is she expecting you, mister? Everybody's pretty busy today."

"Yes, son."

The "son" was inadvertent. It was not apparently resented. Bernie followed the boy along a corridor. They went past double doors marked "Studio A" and with a red-illuminated sign reading "On the Air." They passed "Studio B," which apparently was not on the air. The boy knocked on a door and opened it partway. He said, "A Mr. Simmons, Miss Osborne. Says you're expecting him."

Janet Osborne said, "Yes, Billy." Her voice was a little flatter than Bernie remembered it. He went into a medium-size office and Janet stood up behind a desk —an assistant-size desk, Bernie thought. He said, "Good morning, Miss Osborne." She was just as fair and slim and attractive as she had been Saturday. She was wearing a black dress today. "I'm sorry to barge in on you. It's probably a hectic day here."

"Yes," she said. "It is a—a confusing day. And I suppose that's why you've come, isn't it?"

"A way of putting it," he said, and moved a chair a little so that, sitting in it, he would face her across the desk. "I'm sorry about Mr. Carter, Miss Osborne."

"We're all sorry."

"And you're all being bothered, I suppose. Policemen all over the place, probably."

"There've been men in his office," Janet said. "And up on twenty-one, I think. They haven't gotten around to me much."

"Twenty-one?"

"The twenty-first floor. Where the executive offices are. Mr. Graham's. He's president of IBC, you know.

And Mr. Barnes. And the boardroom's there. And Mr. Willis has an office up there."

Bernie Simmons said he saw. He said, "The police think Mr. Carter's television set may have shorted out. The one he was using up at the Streeters' Saturday. And that he may have got a fatal shock from it."

"That was on the morning news, Mr. Simmons."

"Yes, I gather it was. He had the set turned on on the terrace up there. Listening to the news, as I recall it. Heard something on the news he didn't like, I thought. I just—well, I'd like you to check my memory if you don't mind."

"There was a new anchorman Saturday night. Clay didn't—well, like his approach. A Mr. Latham. Clay had worked with him years ago in Vietnam. When Clay was writing for *Manhattan*. He thought—well, that Mr. Latham had switched sides. As a matter of fact—" She did not finish. Bernie waited.

"Nothing that matters, Mr. Simmons. Yes, he listened to our seven o'clock newscast Saturday evening. The battery just held out."

"Yes, I remember that. And he went over and plugged it in. It seemed to be working all right then. Anyway, the charge light went on, as I remember it."

"Yes. It seemed all right to me. But I don't know much about electrical things."

"Neither do I," Bernie said. "An electric toaster is about my speed. And sometimes I even manage to jam *it* up."

She smiled faintly. Her face—her very attractive face—had seemed stiff before. Had seemed set, as if it were a face she was hiding behind.

She said, "Mine does too," and the faint smile disappeared.

"He left it plugged in until we'd eaten Paul's

steaks, way I remember it. Paul brought it up just as we were leaving. Had Mr. Carter forgotten it, do you suppose?"

"He wouldn't have for long. He always had it with him. When he first made me his assistant he had a bigger one. Heavier. He always had that one with him too, I think."

"You saw a good deal of him, Miss Osborne? Outside the office, I mean."

"We had dinner together now and then. During these last few months. He was fun to be with, Mr. Simmons. Just dinners and things like that. Sometimes to places where we could dance. He—he was a good dancer."

Did her voice break a little there? Or did she merely hesitate momentarily?

"Mr. Streeter brought the television set up to the car," Bernie said. "Came around the house, as I remember it. Did Mr. Carter put it in the trunk, as you recall it?"

"No, just on the floor behind the front seat."

"And then he drove you home. You live downtown, I understand."

"Yes. Off Washington Square. But we didn't go straight there. He wanted me to see his house. It's up on—"

"Yes," Bernie said. "I was up at his house this morning. Getting underfoot, the police think. As I suppose I tend to. Quite a place, Carter's."

"Unexpected," she said. "His grandfather bought it years ago, he told me."

"Did he show you around the house, Miss Osborne?"

Rather to his surprise, she smiled again. "Show me

98

the bedrooms, you mean? No, Mr. Simmons. We just sat in the living room and had nightcaps. And talked. For about forty-five minutes or an hour, at a guess. Then he drove me downtown. And, Mr. Simmons, I didn't invite him in."

She continued to smile. The smile faded out just as Bernie's answered it.

"When you and Mr. Carter went into his house," Bernie said, "do you happen to remember whether he took the television set into the house with him?"

"The 'gimmick,' he always called it. No, I don't think so. I'm pretty sure he didn't."

"Left it in the car? Do you happen to remember whether he locked the car? The car doors, I mean."

She shook her head.

"You mean he didn't?"

"I mean I don't remember, Mr. Simmons."

He nodded his head. He said, "You see, the police think somebody tampered with the set. They wonder who had access to it after he put it in the car. Through the next day, of course. Besides Mr. Carter himself."

"What you're saying is, I did," Janet said. "Is that what you're saying, Mr. Simmons? Is that why you came here? To find out if I did something to the set so it would kill Clay? Clay and I were friends. Do you think I—"

She stopped with that because Bernard Simmons was shaking his head and smiling at her. After she had stopped, he said, "Take it easy, lady. No, I'm not accusing you of anything. I'd have brought someone with me if I'd had that in mind. And warned you. All right?"

Again she smiled faintly. The smile relaxed her face. She said, "Would it have taken long? To tamper with the gimmick, I mean?"

Bernie thought only a few minutes. Not by somebody who knew what he was doing and how to do it . . .
he said, "Mr. Carter could have done it himself, of
course. Any time that night. Any time Sunday. Probably he—"

This time it was she who shook her head and
interrupted.

"Not ever!" Janet said. All the flatness had gone
out of her voice. "Not Clay ever! He—he loved being
alive. Loved fighting for things. Why, only yesterday—"

Evidently, she told Bernie Simmons, Clayton Carter had come down to the office the day before. He
sometimes did on Sundays. He had dictated a memo
and left a note on her desk asking her to have the memo
transcribed and sent upstairs. "Up to Mr. Willis. Wait
a minute."

She opened the top drawer of her desk and took a
flimsy out of it. "Copy" was printed across the sheet.
She slid the flimsy across the desk and said, "Read it,
Mr. Simmons."

"Memo to Godfrey Willis," Bernie read. "Latham's Saturday broadcast was totally out of line and
against network policy. I know I approved your suggestion we take him on but I was nuts. Could it be
somebody planted him on you—by slipping in the back
door when we locked the front? I will urgently advise
Graham not to sign the Latham contract until and unless his function here is unequivocally defined and
agreed to. Will call you tomorrow when I get in, but
am herewith putting my position on record. Cc: Mr.
Graham."

The initials "C.C." were typed at the bottom.

Bernie slid the carbon back across Janet Osborne's
desk.

"You see," she said, "he planned to come in this morning. Mr. Willis comes in earlier than Clay did. His secretary says around nine-thirty most mornings."

"And Mr. Carter? When did he usually come in?"

"About"—she looked at the watch on her wrist—"about now." Bernie looked at his own watch. It was ten minutes after eleven. He nodded. He said, "Godfrey Willis, Miss Osborne?"

"Mr. Willis is in charge of programs. He suggested the network take Ronald Latham on as a newscaster. Oh, Clay approved, of course. As the memo says. He told me he'd known Latham for a long time. He didn't know—well, how much Latham had changed sides. Gone over to B.I. or the Administration. Or both. Turned into a patsy, if you know what I mean."

Bernie knew what she meant. He also knew that objectivity in news reporting is an illusion. Good reporters know too much. What they know seeps into their reports, only sometimes by intention.

"B.I.?" he said.

"Bartwell Industries," she told him. "They tried to buy IBC out a year or so ago. To 'merge' with it, Clay told me once. The way a fox might merge with a chicken, Clay said it would have been. He and some of the other directors stopped it."

"Bartwell Industries," Bernie repeated. "Busy octopus, isn't it? Nora told you they're planning to take over the publisher she works for, didn't she? When you and she were talking Saturday night. Both of you sort of letting your hair down, she thought. Not a thing Nora does often."

"Nor I. I liked your Nora, Mr. Simmons. It is a big octopus."

"Gets fat on Navy overruns," Bernie said. "Would

like to add people's minds to their millions apparently. You worked there once, Nora tells me."

"Only in the stenographic pool," Janet said. "Filling in sometimes when regular secretaries were off. Nothing to do with the reaching out of tentacles. Just rather dull, really. 'In answer to your letter of the twenty-third.' That sort of thing."

"More interesting here, I'd think. More going on."

"Much more interesting. Especially during the last—"

She did not finish. She seemed to look beyond him.

"I've taken up enough of your time," Bernie Simmons said, and started to get up from his chair. But then he sat down again, and said there was one thing more.

"When you were talking to Nora," he said, "you said something about a feeling you had met Paul Streeter before, but couldn't remember where or when." He shook his head. "I sound to myself like a—oh, song? Song title?"

"Song title," she told him. "Before my time, but—the way I know, my father had a record of it and played it a lot. The words were about new things—happenings—seeming to be familiar. As though they'd happened before. A quirk in the mind—déja vu, that is. Did I mention that to Nora? That I had a feeling I'd met —seen, anyway—Dr. Streeter somewhere before?"

"Apparently."

"I did when I first saw him. But it—oh, faded out. Just that quirk, probably."

"Happens to everybody," Bernie said, and this time he did stand up. He said, "Thanks for helping about the migration of the gimmick, Miss Osborne." He crossed to the door and partly opened it, but then turned back. "Oh," he said, "give my best to Phil Whitmore, next time you run into him. Quite a guy, Phil is."

He went out without waiting for a response. He found a telephone booth in the lobby.

The roof hadn't fallen in, Mary Leffing told him at the office. But Captain Stein would like Mr. Simmons to give him a ring. Captain Stein had come up with a few things he thought he and Mr. Simmons ought to talk over.

7

Ronald Latham did the newscast at seven that evening. It had been a dull news day. The Senate had failed, by a margin of three votes, to override the Presidential veto of a bill to grant Federal aid to impoverished school districts in certain states. The President felt that Congress had acted irresponsibly in appropriating the half-million dollars stipulated. The House had passed and sent to the Senate a supplementary appropriation of five hundred million for the Department of Defense.

Latham was factual in reporting these routine happenings of the day. The defense appropriation was, of course, a triumph for the Administration. But so, obviously, was the vote sustaining the veto, although two Democratic senators from the Deep South had deserted the President on the issue.

Latham made no overt editorial comment.

When Ronald Latham said, "And that is the news tonight," and shuffled papers together—he had been reading from a teleprompter, but papers would give viewers a pleasant feeling of immediacy, as if he had just written all the news he was reporting—Janet got up from her desk in Studio B, from which she could watch the news tickers and, if they sounded, hear the alarm bells. They had not sounded that evening; there had been no bulletins to send to Latham's desk during commercial breaks.

She was done for the day. And tomorrow and the day after tomorrow both were vague. The reorganization of the IBC news department was up in the air. (Up on the twenty-first floor, at any rate.) Her job might be; it might blow out of a twenty-first-floor window.

From Madison, she walked across to Fifth with a downtown bus in mind. Plenty of buses were trundling down Fifth Avenue. All of them were destined to turn off at Twenty-third. It was smotheringly hot, and she —why, she thought, I'm tired, more exhausted than I can remember ever being before. And there was a cab with its roof light on.

So it was not quite seven-thirty when she climbed the stairs to her apartment. They were hot stairs, and she climbed through hot and stagnant air. Lillian was due today, she thought. I hope she came. I hope her mother didn't have another attack. I hope if she came, she left the air conditioning on when she left. She's so terribly careful about my electricity, which she always calls "the electric."

Lillian, who came down from Harlem twice a week for four hours a day, at three dollars an hour plus subway fare, had left the air conditioning on. It was not cool in the apartment; it was merely not as hot as it was outside. People like the Streeters are the lucky ones, she thought. In the country, it cools off in the evenings. It was cool on their terrace Saturday evening. I don't want to think about Saturday evening.

Lillian had filled the ice bucket. Lillian was a godsend.

Janet made herself a gin and tonic, heavy on ice and Schweppes, light on gin. She sat on a chair near the window air conditioner and tried not to think about Saturday evening. Monday wasn't anything to think about, either. Would they keep Ronald Latham on in the seven o'clock spot? Would she want to stay on as his assistant? After working with Clay? For that matter, would they want her to? All snafu, she thought. Everything's snafu. How can any man's hair be that red? Now I think about it, I'm pretty sure Clay didn't lock the car doors when we got out at his house. It seems so long ago that we got out of the car in front of that house of his. How could anybody know that the gimmick would be in that car in front of that house?

Sipping her drink, beginning to cool off a little, she thought of an answer to her mind's last question. Dozens of people, probably. Dozens at least knew that he took a portable TV set with him almost everywhere he went. And knew where he lived, or could look it up in the book. But could they? Or did Clayton Carter have an unlisted number?

She put her drink down on a table and crossed the living room to the telephone stand and got the Manhattan directory off the shelf under the phone. She flicked through the Cs. There were a great many Carters. Yes, there was "Carter, Clayton." The address was on Riverside Drive.

Any number of people could have known he was going up to the Streeters' Saturday afternoon. He always left word at the office as to where he could be reached.

She turned to go back to her chair and her drink. Then she saw a slip of paper half hidden under the base of the telephone. She pulled it out and read what was written on it in pencil.

"Man came to fix Phone, Lillian." Lillian always signed her name in full; she always had her own way with capital letters.

To fix phone? But there hasn't been anything wrong with the telephone. I haven't asked to have it fixed. Not for months, anyway. Why should they send somebody to fix it? It's been all right.

She lifted the receiver. She got the dial tone. All right now, at any rate. She went back to her chair and her diminished drink. She lifted the glass to her lips and the telephone blared at her. Her arm jumped and the glass jumped with it. A little of the gin and tonic sloshed out of the glass onto the table. It's never rung so loud before, she thought. Maybe the bell's what they came to fix. She went to the telephone and said "Hullo" into it.

"Good," Phil Whitmore said. "You sound more or less all of a piece. Have you had dinner?"

"More or less is right," Janet said. "I don't know if I'm up to dinner."

"You're damn well up to dinner," he told her. "Half an hour? Hugo's?"

She hesitated. The day had been crowded with people. But the apartment seemed barrenly empty. She said, "Well—" She said, "But not Hugo's tonight."

"Wherever you say."

Did he know Julio's? In Washington Place? A few doors off the Square? "It will be quieter there."

"Half an hour," he said. "I'll pick you up."

"It's only a block from here," she told him. "Suppose I meet you there? At—" She looked at her watch. "At about half-past. All right?"

"However you want it, Jan. Don't get mugged on the way."

She promised to try not to get mugged on the way. She showered and changed to a white-and-aqua print. It would be absurd to meet Phil in office black—mourning black. Would Julio's be air-conditioned? If not, there would be the garden, with its little trickling fountain.

When she was dressed, she looked out a window and realized it would not be the garden. Rain was falling, in a somewhat halfhearted fashion. She carried an umbrella down the stairs with her. But when she left the house she found that she would not need to put the umbrella up.

The rain had stopped. The man on the other side of the street, who was walking slowly toward the Square, apparently had not noticed this. His large black umbrella still was up. The man was only a pair of trousered legs under it. Behind him, the westering sun slanted light through Waverly Place. He seemed not to notice that, either. Of course, some people leave umbrellas up to dry after rain stops.

She reached the Square before the man with the umbrella reached it. He had stopped and tilted the umbrella back over his shoulder and was looking up at a building. For a house number, of course. And he still didn't realize the rain had stopped.

She turned right, crossed the street and walked the short block to Washington Place. Not hurrying. She had allowed herself ten minutes for a walk which could be dawdled in five. To get out of a so-empty apartment?

Or to be waiting when Phil Whitmore reached the restaurant? As she turned again to her right, she saw that the man with the umbrella, still only a pair of trousered legs under it, had given up looking for his street number and was coming, slowly, along Washington Square West. She walked the length of the apartment house on the corner and past somebody's town house and into Julio's—the "Original Julio's." Perhaps, she thought, I should have told Phil about the "Original."

Philip Whitmore was not visible in the restaurant. But it still lacked five minutes of eight-thirty. She sat, in the attitude of one who merely perches for a moment, at a table by a window through which she could see the street.

The man with the umbrella was on the other side of Washington Place. His back was to her, and again he was obviously looking for a house number. Probably had wanted an address in Washington Place, not Waverly Place, all the time. Yes, he had found what he was looking for. He went up four red-stone steps and into the vestibule at the top of them. He put down his umbrella as he went into the vestibule.

A taxi pulled up in front of Julio's, and Phil Whitmore got out of it. It was precisely eight-thirty. Trust Phil to be exactly on time. And trust his right shoulder to be slightly—and so familiarly—higher than his left, as he stood beside the cab to pay off the driver. There was, obscurely, something comforting in the remembered slight irregularity of his shoulders.

She stood up and was conscious that she was smiling at Phil Whitmore as he came into the restaurant. She had not especially planned to smile.

He came into the restaurant and stopped, facing

her. He did not say anything for a moment, but merely looked at her, intently, examiningly. She felt the smile stiffening on her lips. Then Phil Whitmore nodded slowly and smiled at her and said, "Hi." She said "Hi" to him, and the smile still on her lips did not feel stiff any longer.

A man with black hair, wearing a deep red blazer, came up to them and said, "Good evening; two?" and led them to a table for two, against the wall deep in the restaurant. There were not many people in Julio's at eight-thirty on that Monday evening. Phil ordered drinks—very dry martinis—for both of them. He looked across the table at her, and again his eyes were intent. It was, she thought, as if he were measuring her face. For the first time in many hours, amusement crept into her mind.

"Yes," she said, "it's me, Phil. Janet Osborne. And all of a piece. Pretty much all of a piece, anyway."

He smiled at that and nodded again. "I just had to be sure," he said. "At a guess, you've had quite a day. Lots of people asking lots of questions."

"Lots of people," she said. "But mostly upstairs. On the twenty-first. Where the brass has its offices. Mr. Graham. Mr. Willis. People like that. Only Mr. Simmons asked me questions. About Clay's television set, mostly. Of course, the whole shop is—jangled. Wondering—oh, what's going to happen next. To the news department. But—I don't really know. To the whole show. To the network, it felt like today. And especially to—"

A waiter brought drinks. He also brought menu cards, handwritten in purple ink. "Later," Phil said. "Unless the kitchen—?"

"The kitchen remains open, signor. At Julio's there is never hurry."

They sipped from their glasses. Martinis are not always native to Italian restaurants. Julio's did them well enough. A little too much vermouth, Phil thought. But vermouth is, after all, a wine.

"And especially to?" Phil said. "WIBC itself?"

"There was just—oh, buzzing. In the air, if you know what I mean. Yes. About WIBC."

"I've been nosing around a little. Our television department's pretty savvy. WIBC's license renewal comes up in a month or so, apparently. Routine renewal is the usual course. Only, this time maybe not. There's a rumor floating around, our boys tell me. Just rumors, they say."

He stopped to sip from his glass.

"That's all," he said. "Just a floating rumor. They haven't been able to tie it to anything. Or anybody. Only that somebody is maybe going to make a counter-application. Charge that the present management isn't providing the proper public service. Is violating what they call the fairness doctrine."

"It was meant well," she said. "I suppose it was. A chance for both sides."

"Things can get twisted," he told her. "If we give power to twisters. The White House isn't too fond of IBC, you know. It isn't too fond of the *Chronicle,* either, come to that. But newspapers don't need a Federal license. We didn't have to support the Republicans in the last election. And didn't. And got our Washington bureau bugged, of course. In the interest of national security. But we don't have to have a license to go on publishing. Just a second-class mail permit."

He paused to drink. "Of course," he said, "they haven't got around to that yet. Give them time and I wouldn't—" He stopped, seeing he was not being listened to.

Janet, sitting so she faced up the restaurant, was looking past him. He thought she was looking far beyond him.

"Anyway," she said, "he's found out it isn't raining."

There was only one thing to say to that, and Philip Whitmore said it. He said, "Huh?"

"I'm sorry," Janet said. "A man had his umbrella up when I was coming over. Although it had stopped raining. He just came out of the building across the street. He's put his umbrella down now. If it's the same man, that is." She looked at him again and smiled at him. She said, "I'm really sorry, Phil. My mind wanders. A second-class mail permit?"

"Nothing," he said. "Even they won't try that, I guess. Tell me about your umbrella man."

It was nothing, she told him. Just an oddity. Not even that, really. But she told him about the man who had kept his umbrella open after the rain had stopped.

"Letting it dry out a bit before he furled it," Phil said. "People do, you know."

"Of course."

"Trying to find a street number in Waverly Place and then here in Washington Place. Probably just lost. People do get lost here in the Village."

"Of course, Phil. It wasn't anything. They say the scallopini is good here."

"You never saw his face? You just said he'd put his umbrella down."

"Just now it was too dark, dear. It's getting late. Maybe we ought to order, don't you think?"

He looked, a little absently, at their empty glasses. He raised his glass as a signal and the waiter came. He said, "The same, signor?" and, still abstractedly, Whitmore said, "Please," and that they would order.

They looked at menus. "I forgot to tell him drier," Phil said, and she said it didn't matter and that she thought the scallopini, with anything but spinach.

The waiter brought drinks. He took orders for two veal scallopini, without spinach, with eggplant parmigiana, if available. The waiter said, "Signor, signorina," and went away.

Phil Whitmore said, "A lot of people do get lost in the Village. But on the other side of Seventh, mostly."

She said, "Yes, Phil," and sipped from her glass. "I just happened to see him come down across the street. And it was probably another man entirely. I just saw him from the waist down before. It was a very big umbrella. And he carried it low and tilted forward."

He raised his glass and she raised hers, and they drank. He put two cigarettes between his lips and lighted both and handed one to her. He did this absently, resuming a practice for some months broken off. For several minutes they drank and smoked in silence. She watched his face.

"Forget the umbrella," she said. "It wasn't the FBI behind it."

Awareness came back into his face. "No," he said. "Just a man lost in the Village. A man who thought it was raining when it wasn't."

"It had been. It had stopped. Anyway, how could he see through an umbrella?"

"You could see legs," he said. "So, presumably, could he. See where they were going. He got the better view, if you don't mind my saying so."

"I don't mind, Phil. His were just dark trousers. You're making too much of it. Just a man who forgot to put down his umbrella. Thought he was in one street when he was in another. Nothing I should have bothered you with in the first place."

He said, "All right, Jan." But she thought he was still abstracted. Damn umbrellas, she thought. We used to relax together. This has been a day to relax from. Instead, I've worried him. Last night was spoiled by death; tonight by triviality. Last night I felt torn apart. I want to come back together. I began to wander apart when—

"Since you came home from the office," he said. "Did anything else happen?"

"Happen?"

"Anything out of the way. Anything you don't want to bother me with."

"Nothing. I made myself a drink and tried to crawl into the air conditioner. And then you called. And—" Her mind stumbled over something and her voice stumbled with it.

"And?"

"Nothing. Oh, I just remembered. A man had been in to fix the telephone. Lillian had left me a note about him. When you need them it takes forever. And then when the phone's all right they just—well, pop up. You'd think—"

The intentness in his eyes stopped her. "The phone was all right? You hadn't called for a repairman?"

"It seemed all right to me. No, he just showed up. And told Lillian who he was. And fixed whatever was wrong with it, I guess. Why, Phil? I mean, it's nothing to make anything of."

She stopped because, slowly, he was shaking his head. After a moment, she said, "Oh!"

"Yes," he said. "It could be. It's getting to be quite the thing nowadays. Are you blurting guilty secrets over the telephone, dear?"

"I haven't got any. And I don't blurt. Probably

there was something wrong that the telephone company knew about and I didn't. Something that showed up someplace in the—in something at the company's office."

He said, "Possibly." But there was no conviction in his voice. He finished his drink with one swallow, which was not like him. The waiter brought veal scallopini. There hadn't been any eggplant parmigiana left. He brought peas instead. The peas were canned. On the other hand, they weren't spinach. And the scallopini was very good indeed. Janet discovered that, in spite of everything, she was hungry. Which probably, she thought, is a good sign. Of something.

* * * * *

Bernie Simmons opened the door of his apartment at a few minutes before eleven, thinking that John Stein might well be on the right track but that he would have to go a good deal farther along it before the District Attorney's office could approve a charge of anything against anybody. His telephone rang. He went to it and said, "Yes."

"Bernie? Phil Whitmore. Will you tell me something?"

"Hullo, Seer. Depends on what it is. You or the *Chronicle?*"

"Me. Say it's for the old Alma Mater. Or tell me —hell, that national security is involved."

"All right, Phil. We're riding the same hobbyhorse. Which is off the record. Tell you what?"

"Janet Osborne's a friend of mine. I'm a little worried about her. You asked her some questions today, she tells me. About the Carter business."

"Yes. Is that what's worrying you? It needn't.

We're just trying to keep track of this television set of Carter's. The one that killed him. We have to worry a good many people about a good many things."

"Are you, are the police, having her followed? Having her telephone tapped?"

"Not that I know of. And, yes, I should know. Why, Phil?"

Philip Whitmore told him about the man with the umbrella and about the unsummoned telephone repairman. Bernie said, "Mmmm." He said, "I'm pretty sure it wasn't a policeman behind the umbrella. Or fixing telephones. But I'll check it out. Call you back. You're calling from home?"

Whitmore was calling from a booth on Sixth Avenue. He had just left Janet at her apartment. "And made her promise to chain the door." With luck, he could be at his apartment in twenty minutes. He gave Bernie his telephone number.

Bernie checked it out by calling John Stein at his home, which Stein had just reached. Stein knew of no surveillance on Miss Janet Osborne. And the New York Police Department did not tap telephones without court authorization, which Counselor ought to know.

"Neither do we," Bernie told him. "Happen to know if IBC has a security force, Johnny?"

"Who doesn't nowadays? Sure. Man named O'Brien heads it up. Retired captain, uniformed force. Good man, from what I hear."

"Good wire man, maybe?"

Stein did not know. He could find out tomorrow. He put emphasis on the word "tomorrow."

Bernie agreed with the emphasis. It had been a very long day, following a short night. He could think of no reason why anybody should have Janet Osborne followed or have her telephone tapped. The people she worked for or anybody else. Of course, Godfrey Willis was an executive of IBC. Of course, Willis might think the Osborne girl—very nice girl she seemed to be— might know something which would tie him to Grace Carter. And might blab what she knew on the telephone. So what? He'd let that cat out of the bag already, if there was a bag and a cat. Would Carter's bereaved Siamese learn to adjust, thinking of cats? It was a hell of a time to be thinking of cats.

He had better give Paul Whitmore another ten minutes to get home before calling to tell him that if Janet Osborne was being watched over, it wasn't by the police. Bernie made himself a small nightcap.

Willis, as John Stein thought? Or Willis and Grace Carter, working together to break down á barrier created by her religious beliefs? Simple, that way. Quick and simple, and according to a formula with which policemen and assistant district attorneys were, God knew, familiar. Quick, simple and an easy conclusion to jump to. But with nothing really solid to jump from or to land on. Except that maybe Godfrey Willis had a key to Grace Carter's apartment and that she believed the road to hell was paved with divorce decrees.

He finished his short drink. He dialed the number Philip Whitmore had given him.

Whitmore had got home.

"The answer's no," Bernie told him. "Not the cops. Not our office. And, of course, maybe nobody. But in the morning I'll ask the phone company if they sent a repairman around during the day, for any reason, and if not, I'll see her phone's checked on. Meanwhile, if you happen to call her, it might be an idea not to tell her any dark secrets."

"I don't know any, Bernie. Secrets from whom? International communism? Our buddies, nowadays. Something affecting national security?"

"I don't know what secrets," Bernie said. "I don't know from whom, Seer. I wish I did."

"Happen to catch the eleven o'clock news tonight, Bernie?"

"No. The earthshaking more than usual?"

"About as usual. Everybody bugging everybody. Well, thanks for—oh, one item. Old man Hopkins is retiring from the Federal Communications Commission. Reasons of health. Everybody's been expecting it, actually. Give our boy in the White House another appointment to make. Somebody more in the groove. His groove, that is."

"Meaning?"

"Nothing more than usual. The FCC has the last word on licenses for the broadcasters. Alexander Hopkins was a hangover from the old days. The days of permissiveness. Remember them, Bernie?"

"Fondly," Bernard Simmons said. "And off the record, Phil. Officially, I'm a law-and-order cog."

"Sure. Aren't we all? Thanks again, and I hope you catch him. Clay Carter was quite a guy."

8

THE BLARING OF THE TELEPHONE wakened her. The
extension was on the far side of the wide bed. She
rolled toward it sleepily. There was sleep in her voice
as she answered it. Sleep muffled her "Hullo."

"I waked you up, didn't I?" Phil Whitmore said.
"Sorry, Jan."

She looked at the watch on her wrist. It was ten
after nine. It wasn't too early; it wasn't too late. She
was due at the office around ten—if, of course, she was
"due" at the office at all.

"Still there?" Phil asked her.

"Yes, Phil. And high time I was awake."

"You're going to the office? And—you're all right,
Jan?"

There seemed to be anxiety in his voice. The anxiety was comforting.

"Of course," she said. "Of course to both. Why,
dear?"

"Oh," he said. "Umbrellas and things. You chained

yourself in, I hope. Like you promised?"

"Yes. Not an umbrella all night. Forget the umbrella, won't you? It was—oh, I was just silly. Imagining things."

"O.K. Sure you were. Stand me again tonight, Jan?"

For a moment she hesitated. Then she remembered a right shoulder just perceptibly higher than the left. Then she said, "Yes, Phil. I can stand you again tonight. About seven, say? Look, I've got an office to go to. And clothes to put on first."

"Take a cab. It's going to be another scorcher. And, by the way, that Lillian of yours going to be there today? Because Bernie Simmons is sending a man around to check on your phone. Promised me he would."

Lillian was not due that day. "And—I really have to go to the office. Do you know when this man of Mr. Simmons is coming?"

He did not.

"I can leave the door unlocked, I suppose. Only—"

His "No" was quick, emphatic.

"All right," she said. "I suppose you've thrown away the key I—I gave you?"

"Do you? Do you really?"

"No, I suppose I don't really. Do you suppose you could give it to this man Mr. Simmons is sending?"

"I can try. He could stop by the office and pick it up, maybe. Only, the word is 'lend,' Jan. Not 'give.' "

Again, she felt it closing on her. It was absurd that one small word could make, potentially, so great a difference. "Potentially." That was the word.

"All right, Phil. Lend him your key. Until around seven, then. No, seven-thirty would be safer."

He said, "Take care, darling," and hung up.

Words trick you, Janet thought, as she put the

water on for coffee. I shouldn't have said "your" key. I should have said "the" key. I'm a ninny. But she found she was humming as she went to the shower. She couldn't remember the name of the tune, though.

She did not hurry with her shower. She drank orange juice and coffee without hurry. Ten-thirty would be time enough. Things never really started until Clay got in, usually around eleven. How the mind keeps on running in familiar grooves! Clay wouldn't be coming in. She had a cigarette with her second cup of coffee. A yellow dress? No, yellow is a cheerful color. The dark blue linen, then. Why do some dresses look so much better in shops than they do when you get them home?

She put a face on carefully. She put on the blue dress. Oh, well, she would change to a different one before Phil came to pick her up at seven-thirty.

It was a few minutes after ten when, her door safely locked behind her, she went down the four steps from vestibule to sidewalk. She stopped on the last step and looked intently at the tall, lean man walking toward her from Sixth Avenue—the bare-headed man with just a touch of gray showing at the temples of his brown hair. "Becoming" gray. What was Dr. Paul—?

The man smiled, suddenly, and stopped in front of her.

"Why, hul*lo*," he said. "Hullo-hul*lo*."

He was not Paul Streeter. He was just a man who, for a moment, had looked like Paul Streeter. He was a man she could not remember ever having seen before.

"You *are* Janet Osborne, aren't you?" he said. "Don't tell me you're not. Cocktail party at the Campbells'. About a year ago." He looked at her intently, obviously awaiting recognition. He said, "Robert Coppell?" He continued to look at her hopefully. But slowly his expectant smile faded. "Doesn't strike a note?" he said.

She shook her head, regretfully. She said, "Mr. Coppell? I'm afraid I don't—"

"I see you don't," he said. "You're not so easy to forget. But there it is, isn't it? You do remember the party, don't you? Big brawl sort of do. Penthouse? Terrace? You were with somebody. Bill somebody, I think."

"Phil," she said. "Yes, of course I remember the party. Big. Confusing. So many people, met so fast. I'm not good at that sort of thing, Mr. Coppell. I'm terribly sorry."

"No need to be. Only, from the way you looked at me at first—well, I'm forgettable and you're not. Leave it there, and have a good day, Miss Osborne. Nice to have seen you again. And I assure you it is again."

He raised a hand in salute, and the smile came back to his lips. Now, Janet thought, it is a rueful smile. I should have pretended, she thought. It would have been considerate to pretend. But I'm no good at—

"Miss Osborne? Miss Janet Osborne?"

This man was shorter and thicker. She had not noticed him until, standing in front of her, he spoke. She had been looking after the tall, lean man striding on toward the Square. So that was all—

"Miss Osborne? Happened to overhear your friend speak your name."

"Oh. Yes, I'm Janet Osborne."

"Detective Carr. D.A.'s office. Assistant District Attorney Simmons? Check on your telephone?"

"Of course. Did you get the key?"

He said, "Key?" and shook his head. Then he said, "Here, you'd better look at this." This, taken out of his jacket pocket, was a gold-colored shield, with a number on it; with NYPD on it.

"You just caught me," she said. "We were trying to arrange about a key. Come on, I'll let you in."

She climbed the narrow stairway to her apartment door, and Detective Carr followed her. He said on the way up, "Mr. Simmons said tell you the phone company has no record of any service on your telephone, requested or sent, since you had it installed."

Inside, she pointed to the living-room phone. She said, "Will it take long? I'm supposed to be at my office."

He had already taken a small tool—a screwdriver, she thought—and was working on the phone. He said, "Mmmm," and then, "Couple of minutes," and took the bottom off the telephone. He said, "*Uh*-huh," and took something out of the telephone and put it in his pocket. He said, "Extension, Miss Osborne?" and she said, "Yes. Bedroom," and pointed. He went into the bedroom. She was glad she had taken the time to make up the bed.

He came out very quickly. He said, "Use the phone this morning, Miss Osborne?"

"A friend called."

"Hope it wasn't private," Carr said. "Because it wouldn't have been. Mind if I use it?"

He did not wait for an answer to a question obviously without meaning. He lifted the receiver and spun the dial. After a few seconds, he said, "Mr. Bernard Simmons, please. Detective Carr." He waited again and then said what he had said before. Then he said, "Carr, Mr. Simmons. The Osborne job. The answer's yes. Common enough type. Kind everybody uses." He paused for a moment. He said, "Well, damn near everybody, Counselor. Yes, I'll see that it's printed. Waste of time, hundred to one. I'll bring it in and—wait a second, Counselor. The lady wants to talk to you."

Janet had crossed the room and was gesturing at Detective Carr. She took the receiver he held out to her. She said, "Janet Osborne, Mr. Simmons. Nothing at all important, really."

"Yes, Miss Osborne?"

"Yesterday. When you were asking me about Mr. Carter's television set."

"Yes. You've remembered something?"

"Not about that. Not about anything important. Just, that feeling I had that I'd seen Dr. Streeter somewhere before. Before last Saturday, I mean. The feeling I mentioned to Miss Curran and you asked about."

"It's come back to you? Sort of thing that does, sometimes."

"No. Just that the man I thought I remembered wasn't Dr. Streeter at all. Just a man who looked like him. A little like him, anyway. A man named Coppell. I met him at a cocktail party a year or so ago. I got the two confused, was all."

"And suddenly remembered today that it wasn't Paul you remembered—almost remembered—but this other man?"

"Well, it came to that. You see—"

She told him about meeting Robert Coppell in front of the apartment house. Bernie Simmons said he saw. He said, "When you saw him this morning, you did remember meeting him at this party?"

"Not really. I'm not good at remembering faces. When he was quite a way off I thought he was Dr. Streeter. No, I don't actually remember him at the Campbells' party. But he must have been there. He remembered me."

"You do remember the party?"

"Oh, yes. Kenneth and Ruth Campbell throw them once a year or so. And invite everybody they know. And they seem to know a lot. Not the kind of party you forget. Or remember in much detail."

Bernie Simmons said he knew what she meant. "An everybody-in-one-fell-swoop party," he said.

"I shouldn't have bothered you with it," she said. "It was just that Detective Carr had you on the line. I know it doesn't mean anything. Except that things like that—well, sort of itch in your mind. There was a tap on my telephone?"

"Yes."

"Who would put it there? And why, Mr. Simmons?"

Bernie Simmons said he didn't know. He said they would try to find out.

* * * * *

Bernie was mildly glad that Janet Osborne's mind had been cleared of the burr of a half memory. Such burrs can be irritating. Janet had seemed like a nice girl. Also, she had a rather good forehand. Not as good as Nora's, perhaps. But there he had to admit prejudice. Thinking of Nora Curran tempted him to call her up. Just to—oh, just to tell her that a young woman she had met only once had got a burr of half memory cleared out of her mind. And drag her, almost certainly, out of the depths of somebody's manuscript. He looked at his own In basket, which bulged. After all, he and Nora were having dinner together in—he looked at his watch—nine hours or so.

He began to take papers out of the In basket. Nothing either of urgency or interest. Papers that required initials. Who put a bug on Janet Osborne's telephone? And why?

A member of the security force of IBC? If so, on

whose instruction? Godfrey Willis's, because she might know too much about Willis and Grace Carter? It seemed a little far-fetched. Unless Willis thought Carter might have known too much and told what he knew to his assistant. Confidential assistant, call it. How confidential?

Bernie couldn't answer that one. There were a lot of them he couldn't answer. It would be simple if Johnny Stein's theory turned out to be accurate, and provable. Way cleared for marriage to, according to Johnny, a most attractive, no longer religion-bound mistress. And a rich one, now. Owner, among other things, of almost a third of the corporate stock of Independent Broadcasting. Thirty percent of the stock, John had said. Enough, with what he already owned, to give Willis—no. Willis didn't own any stock in IBC. That had been verified yesterday. Willis just worked there. At, to be sure, upward of sixty thousand a year. Of course, Peter Graham, president of IBC, made more than twice that.

I don't know these people, Bernie thought. They are faceless; names on file cards of my mind.

Ronald Latham is a faceless name. Anchorman on a news show on Saturday nights. Or only one Saturday night. The sort of man who would kill to protect a job? More questions; fewer answers. Let's hope Stein's theory holds water.

His telephone rang. "Captain Stein is on the line, Mr. Simmons."

"Morning, John. There was a tap on Miss Osborne's phone."

Stein already knew that. Detective Carr had been through to him.

"And the man Paul Streeter Miss Osborne half remembered. Turns out he was a man named Coppell whom she'd met at a cocktail party. Looks like Paul, apparently."

He told Stein about Janet Osborne's chance encounter with Robert Coppell. John Stein said, "Mmmm."

"We've been on to O'Brien," Stein said. "Security chief at IBC. Sean O'Brien. Very Irish. Happens his mother was Jewish, according to department records. Father insisted on the Sean, at a guess. Wearing of the green. Anyway—"

Anyway, O'Brien's security force at IBC consisted of eight men, five of them licensed private investigators, with pistol permits; the other three in the category of night watchmen. "Mostly to protect equipment. To keep out right-wing fanatics, O'Brien says. Who want, and I quote, 'to protect national security by getting IBC off the air.' Whimsical type, O'Brien."

"Well—any of them tried it, Johnny?"

"One or two incidents, O'Brien says. IBC stayed on the air. Point is, no wire men O'Brien knows of. Never tapped anything as long as O'Brien's been there. Never been asked to. Wouldn't have done it if he had been asked. Wouldn't stand for anything illegal."

"Vanishing breed," Bernie said. "Anything else I ought to know, John?"

"Mrs. Grace Carter's gone shopping. Saks Fifth Avenue, last we heard. We can't see Mr. Willis until late this afternoon. Couple of routine questions we want to ask him about the administrative setup at the network. He's got a lunch date at one, his secretary says. With an independent producer, she says. Probably won't be back at the office until three-thirty. Maybe four."

"And?"

"One of the boys from precinct is having a little

chat with Irene—Irene Folsom, that is. Mrs. Carter's maid. About this and that. Keys and things. Anyway, I hope he is. Hope she's chatty. And—hold it a minute, Bernie. Something's coming through."

Bernie held it for more than a minute. Grace Carter had company on her shopping expedition. She probably would have it at lunch, if she stayed out for lunch. If, say, she had an engagement for lunch. O'Brien probably would know if one of the men on his security force was experienced in electronic surveillance. Of course, he might not tell all he knew.

"Yes, John?"

"Cyril Johnson's been slugged," Stein said. "Carter's valet, or whatever Carter called him. Called police emergency. Got switched to precinct. Lane's on his way up."

"Johnson called himself?"

"Way I get it. Sounded a little groggy to the man catching at precinct. Fuzzy. Something about a telephone man. Lane will sort it out. Call you back when I know something."

Bernie cradled his telephone and thought, Now what the hell? There was no immediate response to his query.

The administrative setup at IBC. About which Johnny Stein wanted to talk to Godfrey Willis. Detectives from the precinct squad and Paul Lane and another man from Homicide North had pretty thoroughly gone into that the day before, and Stein had filled Bernie in during that afternoon and over dinner. Bernie had noted names down on a memo pad.

Godfrey Willis's name led all the rest, since it was around him Stein was forming a pattern in his mind. Vice-president in charge of programming. Had been for three years. With IBC for five years. An executive with another network before that. No known ownership of stock in IBC. Age, somewhere in late forties. Born in California. Widower for some years. As director of programming, probably would have numerous contacts with independent producers. Might very well, obviously, negotiate over lunch.

The mind scatters. Cyril Johnson had seemed like a nice guy. Banged up, apparently, but not so badly he couldn't telephone the police. Hope that long, talkative —and bereft—cat of Carter's didn't get banged up too. Siamese cats had once been palace guards in Siam. Where did that scrap come from? And is there any truth in it? The mind scatters.

Peter Graham, president of IBC. In his early sixties. One of the most vigorous leaders in the defense of the broadcasting industry against Administration efforts to put a leash on it. Relatively minor shareholder in IBC. Long career in broadcasting. Graduate of MIT. Annual salary, one hundred and fifty thousand, plus stock bonuses. The one who would approve Ronald Latham's contract as news anchorman. If it was approved, of course.

J. Livingston Barnes, chairman of the board. Right kind of name for the job, anyway. Owned roughly twenty percent of the IBC stock. Less, apparently, than Clayton Carter had owned. Why hadn't Carter been board chairman?

Twenty percent of the shares registered to "Consolidated Communications," whatever that might be. The rest of the shares scattered. Far and wide, probably. Like my mind.

His telephone rang. Stein with information about Cyril Johnson and whatever it was about a "telephone man." Quick work, if—

"A Dr. Streeter, Mr. Simmons. Dr. Paul Streeter."

9

BERNIE SAID, "MORNING, PAUL," and Paul Streeter said, "Hell of a thing about Clay Carter."

Bernie agreed it was a hell of a thing.

"Fine man," Streeter said. "Best man IBC had, by a long shot."

Bernie said, "Yes, Paul," and waited.

"Just heard about it this morning," Streeter said. "We drove up to Vermont Sunday to get out of the heat. Got back last night. Read about Clay this morning. Damnedest thing. Is it true somebody killed him?"

"Yes, apparently."

"By shorting out that TV of his? The one he was using Saturday?"

"That's the way it looks, Paul. The way the police think it was."

"That harmless little gadget," Paul Streeter said.

"Electricity isn't ever harmless. Just usually domesticated."

"It seemed—well, inoffensive when I took it up from the terrace. Damn it all, I should have left it there. Let him forget it."

"I doubt he would have, Paul."

"All right when I unplugged it," Paul said. "All charged up, apparently. I happened to hit the knob sort of thing that turns it on when I was pulling the cord out of the socket. It began to make those warming-up noises and the screen lighted up. So I turned it off. It was all right then." He paused for a moment. He said, "Lucky for me it was, probably. I might have got the jolt Clay got."

"Not unless you were grounded, they tell me," Bernie said. "Had your feet in the water, as the police assume Carter did. Anyway, the set was all right when you handled it. Apparently somebody bugged it later."

"Bugged?"

"I've got bugs on my mind, one way or another. Tampered with it, I mean."

"You're sure somebody did? That it wasn't merely an accidental malfunction?"

"The police seem pretty sure, Paul."

"According to the *Chronicle,* the District Attorney's office is cooperating in the investigation," Streeter said. "Probably means you, Bernie."

"We always cooperate," Bernie said. "Glad to know the set was working when you picked it up from the terrace. Narrows it down a little."

Paul Streeter said he had thought it might. He repeated that it was a hell of a thing. "Shook us both up," he added.

Bernie thanked Paul Streeter for calling. And hung up, wondering mildly why Streeter had called. Probably hoping his assurance that Carter's TV had been in working order when he lifted it from the terrace and carried it up to Carter's car would be helpful. Well, it was a minor point worth pinning down.

Bernie went back to his In basket. It didn't produce anything more interesting than it had before. He felt as if he were hanging in space. Space nowadays was full of hanging objects. His telephone rang and brought him back to the solidity of his desk. This time it was Captain John Stein.

"Johnson's got a bump on the head," Stein said. "Also a bruised jaw. Way he tells it to Lane—"

The doorbell of the house on Riverside Drive had rung at a little after eight. Cyril Johnson had just finished eating his breakfast. He had scraped uneaten food out of Mao's dish and put fresh food in it. Even the sound of scraping had not brought the long cat to the kitchen. Mao was still on Carter's bed, waiting. Johnson had gone to answer the door and had opened it.

The man who had rung the doorbell had said, "Telephone repairman," and had come in.

"Why?" Johnson said. "The phone's all right."

"This is the Carter residence, isn't it?" the man said, as Johnson remembered it. "Got an order on it. Where's the phone, boy?"

"Johnson's apparently a careful man," Stein said. "And maybe that 'boy' annoyed him. Anyway, he said he'd have to see some identification. Which is about the last thing he remembers. Apparently, the man hit him on the jaw. Left side of the jaw, so we're looking for a right-hander. Hit him hard enough to knock him off his feet. Falling, he hit his head on a table in the hall. Marble top, the table has, Lane says."

Johnson had been out for around twenty minutes. He had looked at his watch when the doorbell rang and the time had been eight-ten. When he came to, he had looked at it again. Eight-thirty. "A man who keeps track of things, Johnson is," Stein said. "Make a good witness, wouldn't he?"

"Good at identification too, John?"

"This way and that way," Stein said. "Around six feet, Johnson thinks. Maybe a little under. Thickset. Wearing a cap, with the visor pulled down."

"He won't be by now," Bernie said. "The telephones, John? Bugs in them?"

That was the catch. There were four telephone instruments in the ancient house which had been Carter's: a wall phone in the kitchen, phones in the living room and in Carter's bedroom-office, a phone in the room which had been Grace Carter's. "What they call a 'princess' phone in her room."

"Speaking of Mrs. Carter?"

"Gone on to Bonwit's, last we heard. Looking for dresses, Bradbury says. Damn hard not to stand out in a woman's dress department, Brad said. She goes into a fitting room and what's he supposed to do?"

Bernie didn't know what Detective Bradbury was supposed to do. He realized Bradbury might find the situation trying. To get back to Cyril Johnson. Did he think he could pick out a picture of the telephone man? And what had the telephone man done to the four telephones?

"He thinks maybe, but he doubts it. I don't know what was done to the phones. There aren't any bugs in them. And the line isn't tapped where it comes into the house. The telephone company's sending men to check out. And they didn't send a repairman."

"Take bugs out instead of putting them in, John?"

"Now, Counselor, believe it or not, we've thought of that. In our fuzzy-minded way."

Bernie said he was sorry, Captain. He said, "Doctors check out on Johnson's bumped head, John?"

"No. Lane and the precinct men tried to get him to go to the hospital. No soap. 'Refused medical attention,' way it reads in the report. He told Lane he had to wait for the cat."

Bernie said, "Huh?"

"The cat. Siamese. Name of Mao. Seems the man who slugged Johnson left the door ajar when he took off; Mao pulled it the rest of the way open and went out. Johnson's very much upset, Lane says. Has to be around to let Mao in when he comes back."

"Mao will come back, Johnson thinks? Usually does?"

"He doesn't usually get out, Johnson says. Not in front, anyway. Sometimes he's let out behind the house. Where it's fenced in."

"Cats don't much mind fences," Bernie said. "Gone looking for Carter, I suppose. Too bad we can't explain things to them, isn't it?"

John Stein said, "Yeah." Then he said, "Hold it a minute," and Bernie Simmons held it a minute.

"Telephone men showed up," Stein said. "Real ones, this time. They can't be sure, but they think there was a tap on Carter's phones where the cable comes into the house. Marks on the lead-in wire. If there was, the man knew what he was doing."

"And O'Brien says there aren't any wire men on his force?"

"What he says, Bernie. You stirred up anything?"

"Not a damn thing," Bernard Simmons said.

Stein said, "Tut-tut," and hung up.

* * * * *

It was going to be another damn hot day. Hell, it was already a damn hot day, at a little after eleven in the morning. Sometime they'd get around to air-conditioning State Patrol police cars. Maybe. Trooper Fred Turner cruised slowly out of Mt. Kisco in the general direction of Katonah. One way was as good as another. And probably as pointless. Since eight o'clock motorists had been law-abiding. No speeders. No drunks wandering all over the roads. Some days are like that. Some days there doesn't seem much point in being a cop. And some days are too damn hot.

The implacable sun beat down on the police cruiser, and the air coming in through the open windows was stifling air. The sweatband of Trooper Turner's uniform hat felt like an iron band burning into his forehead. There ought to be shade somewhere: a place where he could pull off the road and into the shade and at least take his hat off. Along here somewhere. Sure, Pinetree Lane. And a shady pull-off. Along here somewhere. Sure, Pinetree Lane. And a shady pull-off a hundred yards or so in.

Turner drove into Pinetree Lane. He turned the car by backing into somebody's driveway, and pulled off the narrow blacktop in a shady place with the car facing the highway. If somebody went toward Katonah—or Mt. Kisco, for that matter—at seventy or eighty miles an hour, Turner could pop out and take after him. Not that anybody would. On the Saw Mill River Parkway, sure. But that would be up to the Parkway police. Trooper Turner took his hat off. Here in the shade, there was even a faint breeze. A cold beer would be—you're on duty, fellow. A ten-minute break is one thing. Beer is quite another. You're a New York State trooper, Trooper.

For most of the allowable ten minutes nothing happened, except that Turner got a little more comfortable with his hat off and air stirring through the car. Not cool air, of course. It was, after all, July. But at least the sun wasn't burning its way through the windshield and glaring into the driver's window. Turner took off his sunglasses. Beyond his shaded refuge, sunshine glared at him.

On the highway, a blue sedan bound toward Katonah slowed as if it were about to turn into the lane. But then, it straightened out and went on toward Katonah. Or Brewster. Or Cross River or God knew where. Somebody who had thought he wanted Pinetree Lane and found he didn't. Or thought Pinetree was Grove Road, which was half a mile or so on up. Or—hell—thought the police car was blocking the road? But I'm well off the road. All the room in the world for him to pass. Really stepping on it now, from the sound of his engine.

Turner turned the ignition key of the cruiser and the engine caught. He put his uniform hat on and went into gear.

The car was a good distance up the highway and really moving along. Turner closed up a little and paced the car for a couple of miles. Doing sixty-five, he made it. In a forty-five zone and on a winding road.

Trooper Turner started his siren going. The man in the car ahead didn't hear it. Or didn't want to hear it. Or thought it was a warning for somebody else. Turner stepped the cruiser up to seventy-five and began to close, the siren screaming. The driver of the other car took it in this time. He began to slow. Turner slowed the cruiser.

He was a couple of hundred yards back of the car he was chasing when there was a sign "Warning. Trucks Entering Highway." There were a lot of signs like that, as there were a lot of "Deer Crossing" signs. Deer mostly didn't cross and trucks didn't—

Trooper Turner slammed his foot down on the

brake pedal. Ahead of him, tires screamed on macadam. The truck which had begun to nose its way out of a lane stopped abruptly. But not before it had protruded into the highway in front of the car ahead.

The blue sedan was doing only about forty when the truck nosed out in front of it. It swerved away. The driver was quick; almost quick enough. Not quite enough. There was a rasp of metal, and the sedan bounced away. It bounced across the road, skidding against locked brakes. There was a ditch on the far side of the road and the sedan nosed into it—seemed to burrow into it—and stopped.

Turner, the cruiser stopped just safe of the truck, could see the sedan's driver surge forward in his seat. If he was wearing a seat belt he might be all right, Turner thought, running toward the sedan. The truck was backing farther into the lane as he ran past it. The truck driver stared at him. The truck driver was slowly shaking his head from side to side.

The driver of the sedan had been wearing a seat belt. It had helped. He had not been thrown through the windshield. But he had been thrown forward, over the wheel and against the instrument panel. He did not move when Turner yanked the door open and did not answer when Turner shouted at him. Out cold; at least out cold. Possibly for keeps. No. Breathing. Turner ran back to the cruiser's radio. The Mt. Kisco medical center was only a few miles away. It was only ten minutes or so before Turner heard the ambulance siren.

Turner told the truck driver to stay where he was. "You damn fool!" He went back and eased the door of the sedan open. The driver was a big man—thickset and probably about six feet. Turner couldn't see that he was bleeding much. Only a trickle from his forehead. He was still breathing—and still unconscious. With help sounding its way toward them—professional help—Turner didn't try to move him.

The ambulance men were very careful getting the man out from behind the wheel of the sedan onto a stretcher and into the ambulance. He started to come to just as they were closing the door on him. He said something and the attendant said, "You'll be all right, mister. Just take it easy."

"Case," the man said. "On seat."

Turner had gone over to the ambulance.

"Sure," the attendant said. "We'll take care of that. Just take it easy." He closed the ambulance door.

"He'll make out?" Turner asked.

"Up to the doctors," the man in white said. "Just a concussion, be my guess. Coming out of it already. Said something about a case, near as I could make out. You chasing him, Trooper?"

"Just for speeding," Turner said.

The blue sedan, still half on the roadway, and the ambulance and the police cruiser were blocking the highway. Cars from Katonah and Mt. Kisco were forming lines in either direction. They were beginning to bleat about it. Pretty soon, the more impatient would be walking up to find out about it. Get hold of a wrecker—that was the immediate job of State Trooper Frederick Turner. Get the road cleared.

He started back to the cruiser and stopped. Just maybe—he went back to the blue sedan. It didn't look too much banged up. He got into it.

On the floor next to the driver's seat there was a flat case, thrown to the floor when the car bounced into the ditch. Thrown and sprung open. Turner lifted it to the seat beside him and started to snap it shut. And stopped when he could see into it.

What was in the case were neat stacks of bank-notes, looking crisp and new, with bank bands around them. The shallow case was almost full of neatly packaged bills, and the bill on top of each package Turner could see was a hundred-dollar bill. Turner's response was simple and immediate. Turner would be damned.

The impact which had jarred the flat case to the floor had also sprung the glove compartment open. Inside the compartment was a revolver—a .38. Turner was pretty sure of that. He knew more about sidearms than about hundred-dollar bills. It raised problems; it sure as hell raised problems. The ignition key was firm in the lock on the steering column. But the engine wasn't running. Turned the ignition off when he knew he was going to crash? Wise of him, if so. And very alert of him. Perhaps the ignition had been turned off accidentally when the heavyset man was hurled against the wheel. Anyway—

Turner got out of the blue sedan and had a good look at it. Left front fender bashed in. But still clearing the tire, apparently. He'd know when he tried. Front of the hood fairly deep in what looked to be soft earth. Of course, if the radiator casing had smashed against a buried rock, that would be that. The ditch wasn't a wide one. The rear wheels were inside the shoulder, but not by much. The shoulder was gravel. It didn't seem to be too loose.

Trooper Turner got back into the sedan. You never know till you try. He turned the ignition key. The starter snarled. The engine did not catch. Have to call a wrecker after all. Then the engine coughed. Turner pressed the gas pedal to the floor and let it halfway up again. The engine coughed twice again. Then it roared.

In reverse, the drive wheels spun. But the car

moved a little. Turner let it nose forward for a foot or two and tried reverse again. Again the wheels spun. But then they bit in. Slowly, with reluctance, the blue sedan floundered out of the ditch onto the pavement. Turner turned it toward Mt. Kisco and parked it on the shoulder. The first of the westbound cars crept past. Turner let three cars go on toward Mt. Kisco— or New York City, or wherever—and stopped the fourth. He crossed to his cruiser, with the red light flashing on its roof.

The truck which had caused it all had backed on in toward, as it turned out, a gravel pit. The driver had got out of it and was sitting on shaded grass, smoking a pipe. He got up when Turner drove the cruiser off the road into the lane and pulled it up beside the truck.

"He was going like hell," the truck driver said. "We've got rights like anybody else. Sign down there says—"

"I know what the sign says. Go ahead and get it out of here. And for God's sake, look where you're going."

"Sure," the trucker said. "Like I always do. Way I see it—"

He stopped, because Turner was not waiting to hear how he saw it. He was on his way back to the blue sedan, hoping nobody had walked off with all that money while his back was turned.

Nobody had. The crumpled left front fender cleared the wheel by a reasonable margin. The radiator shield was bashed in, but the radiator wasn't leaking. The bumper—one of the new ones which were supposed to act like bumpers—was still there. It did rattle as he drove the sedan toward Mt. Kisco, but it didn't fall off. Turner stopped at the emergency entrance of the medical center. He carried the attaché case when he went into the emergency ward. He also carried the .38.

He said, "How's he making out?" to the middle-aged nurse's aide behind the desk. "And what have you got on him?"

"Mild concussion, they say. Fully conscious. Just needs to rest a little, doctor says. His name's Pfeiffer, Arnold. Here."

She took a wallet out of the desk drawer and held it out to Turner.

Pfeiffer, Arnold, had a New York State driver's license. He also had a pistol permit. He was a private investigator, duly licensed. The wallet contained the car's registration. The blue sedan was not Arnold Pfeiffer's car. Its registered owner was "ConCom Corp." with an address in the W. 40s, NYC. So Arnold Pfeiffer was legal, and with a legal right to have a thirty-eight-caliber revolver in the glove compartment of the car he was driving.

Of course, he had been driving it too fast. He had a summons coming. And he'd had what looked like a hell of a lot of money in a flat case in the car. No law Turner knew of against carrying a lot of money with you, providing, of course, that it was your own money. Or legal money.

"Up to seeing anybody?"

She would ask Doctor. "Trooper—?"

He filled in the name for her. She used the telephone. She said, "Right in there," and pointed. He said, "Better put these in the safe. Mr. Pfeiffer's property. There's money in the case." He gave her the attaché case and the revolver. She took the revolver as if she expected it to bite her.

There were three empty hospital beds in the room

Turner went into. There was one bed with the heavy-set man propped up in it. He was dressed, except for shoes and jacket. There was a large adhesive bandage over a considerable swelling on his forehead. His blue eyes were open. His blond hair was cut short.

"You're the trooper was chasing me?" Arnold Pfeiffer said. He spoke abruptly. Turner nodded his head. "Look," Pfeiffer said. "There was property in the car. You just leave the car there in the ditch that damned truck pushed me in?"

"The car's out front. And the case you were worrying about's in the safe. So's your gun, Mr. Pfeiffer."

"Got a permit for the gun," Pfeiffer said. "You look in the case, Officer?"

He wasn't abrupt any more.

"It fell off the seat," Turner said. "Got sprung open. Yeah, I saw the money. And I know you've got a license to carry the gun. And that you've got a summons coming. Seventy in a forty-five zone. In one hell of a hurry, weren't you?"

"All right, you caught me. So write it out, Officer."

"Company car, apparently. Something called 'Con-Com,' it says on the license. You work for them, Mr. Pfeiffer?"

"Conover and Comfortobelli," Pfeiffer said. "Incorporated as ConCom. Like—oh, like Sears Roebuck, sort of. Confidential investigations. Yes, I work for them."

"On an errand for them this morning?"

"You can call it that. Confidential, but entirely legal, officer. With the tacit approval of the city police. New York City, that is."

"Jewel recovery?"

Pfeiffer smiled to that. He said, "No comment, Trooper."

"Mind telling me where you were bound in such a rush?"

"Danbury. To meet a man who—well, say, likes to live in Connecticut."

"There are faster roads from New York to Danbury, Mr. Pfeiffer."

"All right. Let's say I like back roads. Any law against it?"

Turner agreed there was no law against preferring back roads to the compulsions of superhighways. He said, "Friday afternoon all right with you? To tell a justice of the peace here in Mt. Kisco why you were going so damn fast? And pay your fine?"

"Unless I can pay it to you and save us both the—"

"No," Turner said. "Don't get any ideas, Mr. Pfeiffer. And take it easy. And if you can't, watch out for highway patrols, O.K.?"

"You came out of nowhere," Pfeiffer said. "Lying in wait somewhere?"

"Just pulled off the road for a couple of minutes," Turner said, and wrote out the summons and gave it to the big, blond, private detective. "You banged the car up a bit, you know. Have to get some body work done. Here's the car key."

He gave Pfeiffer the ignition key to the blue sedan. Outside, he called in before he got a ride back to pick up the cruiser.

10

For Philip Whitmore, "about seven-thirty" meant seven-thirty on the nose. Janet was ready; for five minutes she had been ready. She didn't bother to call down. The dingus didn't really work, anyway. She pushed on the button and heard the click and heard the vestibule door open. She watched Phil come up the stairs, carrying one shoulder a little lower than the other.

At the top of the stairs he did not touch her, although for a moment she thought his hands moved as if to lift toward her. For what seemed a long time, he looked intently at her face. She smiled at him. When he continued to look at her, she said, "Think you'll remember me if you see me again?"

He nodded but not, she knew, in answer to a question which was not a question. Then he said, "Hi. I ever take you to Larry's? Or did anybody else?"

She said, "Larry's?"

"Restaurant uptown," he said. "Near the office.

Used to be more or less a hangout. Not so much now, since the *Blade-Examiner* folded. Funny old place. Not really sawdust on the floor. But you sort of think there is. Want to try it for a change? It's—oh, sort of dim and cool. If anything's cool. Of course, there's always Hugo's."

"Wherever you say, Phil."

She put on her white gloves. His wide mouth went into a wide grin as he watched her put the gloves on, and he shook his head slowly. She laughed, lightly, and went ahead of him down the stairs. A cab was waiting. There was a window sticker which read "Air Conditioned."

"Once you catch them, never let them go," Phil said and opened the door for her.

Larry's was on Forty-fourth Street, just west of Broadway. A bar ran long down one side of a rather narrow room, and it was a busy bar. Only men stood in front of it and, as they walked behind them, Janet felt as if the bar was the bar of a club—a club for men only.

"Tables in the rear," Phil said. "Ladies welcome."

They went down a shallow step into a much wider room, a cool dim room. In the center of the room, a four-bladed ceiling fan revolved slowly. "Just a prop, really," Phil said. "Atmosphere. The place is air-conditioned. Over there all right?"

"Over there" was a heavy wooden table against the wall, its uncovered top glossy. As they walked toward it, Phil guided them so that they did not walk under the lumbering fan. "Thing like that almost fell on me once," he said. "Missed me by inches. Not here. Down south. At somebody's cocktail party. Old, old South."

He pulled out a chair for her. When she was on it, it took both of them to slide it back up to the table.

He slid in the other chair, across from her. A waiter in a dinner jacket, a starched winged collar and a long white apron came up to the table. He walked as if his feet hurt. He said, "Long time no see, Mr. Whitmore," and Janet's polite smile felt as if it were freezing on her lips. Phil said, "Evening, Joseph, it has been a while."

The waiter brought heavy silverware and set the table. He brought heavy place-plates. He said, "Something from the bar, maybe?" They ordered something from the bar. They looked at the menus the waiter had left them.

"It's not a salad sort of place," Phil told her. "Meat and potatoes. Some of the best steaks in town. They carve the roast beef thick. If you want it rare it comes rare. When they say 'prime' they mean prime. The baked Idaho potatoes come from Idaho. One of the few places you can still get mutton chops, if you like mutton chops. The steaks are big. They don't fool around. Thank you, Joseph. We'll order later."

They clicked glasses. Again, he was looking intently at her face. She nodded slowly.

"Yes, Philip," Janet said. "I'm all right. Don't I look all right?"

"You look fine. The roast lamb comes pink, if you order it pink. They do the french fries to order. Your drink all right? They use Tanqueray."

Her martini was fine. It was very cold. It was also about twice martini-size.

"Dear," Janet said, "are you the official pitchman for Larry's? You don't sound like you. I'm really all right." She smiled at him. *"Really,"* she said.

Phil nodded acceptingly. They both sipped from their glasses. Air from the trundling ceiling fan ruffled her hair a little. It was relaxing in this big, only partially filled back room of Larry's. It was relaxing to be sitting across the too-wide table from Philip Whitmore.

"Things settling down at the office?" he said. He spoke lightly, as of some trivial matter.

"A little. Latham's going to anchor 'The News Tonight.' For now, anyway. To read it, that is. Mr. Willis will take over as news director, also for the time being. The job Clay—the job Clay had."

He did not seem to notice her slight hesitation over Clayton Carter's name. He said, "And you?"

"Assist Mr. Willis. It's all pretty tentative. Improvised. And rumors floating. Hiring a man from one of the other networks. CBS, maybe." He raised his eyebrows. "No," she said, "not Cronkite. We're not that size."

"But the hole Clay left is that size?"

"Yes. Just about."

"Tell me about the hole, Jan. What was the setup? Cronkite's called managing editor at CBS. Clay Carter?"

"Pretty much the same, I guess. Shape up the whole thing. Decide what stories to cover. Assign the correspondents to cover them. Decide on policy. Oh— almost all of it. A lot of the writing, too. Some days, most of it. He was a reporter for years, you know. I mean for newspapers."

"And a news service. And for a magazine. Yes. I do know. I'm in the same trade, dear."

"You don't," she said, "need to sound so damn tolerant. So, I'm just a promoted typist."

"All right," Phil said. "Professionals tend to get arrogant. Don't bristle at me. Drink your drink. That's sawdust on the floor. This is all fifty years ago. The turn-of-the-century years ago. Drink your drink, lady."

Again he was looking at her intently. But now he was smiling as he looked. She obediently supplied the floor with sawdust and drank her drink.

The waiter named Joseph came toward them, still walking as if his feet hurt.

"Yes," Phil said. "The same again, Joseph. Then we'll order."

Joseph said, "Coming up, Mr. Whitmore," and took away empty glasses.

"At the turn of the century," Philip Whitmore said, "The last century, it would have been lively. And I—"

"All right. You'd have drunk champagne from my slipper."

"Of course. And changed all your typewriter ribbons."

Joseph brought new drinks. They clicked their glasses together. It was very relaxing in the back room of Larry's. She felt as if she were, indeed, drifting lazily backward to a quieter time. Perhaps it was the extra-size martini. Perhaps no time had been really quiet.

The roast lamb she had ordered pink did come pink; garlic had been used judiciously. The big Idaho potato which came with it was not shrouded in aluminum foil. It had been forked open, not knifed open. It was flakily dry, not drowned in butter. Larry's provided the unsalted butter, left its use to the discretion of the customer. Phil's steak was thick and properly underdone. It seemed to part readily to his knife. The domestic Burgundy was mellow without being sweet. Everything was fine. They did not interrupt the food with conversation.

Even when they had finished, they did not talk much. Phil did say, "Cheesecake?" and she did say she guessed not. The coffee, which Joseph brought in a silver pot, was clear and strong. She accepted the cigarette Phil held out to her and the light he gave her. The slowly revolving fan eddied the smoke between them, then away from them.

It is peaceful here, Janet thought. All the racket, all the confusion, we have left outside. There is no reason to say anything about it. There is no reason to say anything about anything. I feel—I feel as if I had come home to something. Even when he is sitting down, one shoulder is just perceptibly lower than the other. I don't want to go any place else but here. I don't care what news Ronald Latham reads tonight in that actor's voice of his. It will all have floated away by tomorrow.

There was now no intentness in Phil Whitmore's face when he looked across the table at her. People got up and left other tables, and Larry's big back room (with symbolic sawdust on the floor) grew even quieter. The welcome dimness seemed to increase, although no lights were dimmed. It was almost ten when Phil lifted his eyebrows and said, "Well?"

She said, "Yes, I suppose so," and heard her own voice as if it were breaking a spell.

Joseph brought the check and Phil added a tip to the total and signed it and Joseph said, "Thank you very much, Mr. Whitmore."

The bar was still lined as they walked past it, but the men were no longer shoulder to shoulder. Near the end closest to the door, a tall man was standing. They were a step or two beyond him when he turned toward them.

"We do seem to run into each other, don't we, Miss Osborne? And you still don't recognize me, do you?"

149

"Yes, Mr. Coppell. Of course I do," Janet said. She felt as if she should say something else, but there seemed nothing else to say. She walked on.

Coppell looked for a moment at Whitmore, nodded politely to a stranger and turned back to the beer on the bar in front of him.

A taxi was loitering by in West Forty-fourth Street, but Whitmore did not hail it. Instead, he stepped aside a few feet and looked back through the door at the bar. He looked for several seconds before he looked again at Janet. And she felt peace seeping out of her.

"So that's the man you confused with Dr. Streeter," he said. "The man who said his name was Coppell. Coincidence running into him again, wasn't it?"

"Yes, Phil. The man I first thought was Dr. Streeter. The man who remembered me from the Campbells' party."

"Well, the world's full of coincidences, I suppose. People looking like other people. That sort of thing. 'Coppell,' you said?"

"Yes, Phil. Don't tell me he looks like somebody you know."

"I'm afraid I've got to," Phil Whitmore said. "A man who worked on the *Chronicle* for a while a few years back. In the city room, I think. Just before I left the city staff and got the column—the all-knowing seer column. Only, his name wasn't Coppell, then. Ray something or other. Raymond Harkness, I think it was. No—wait a minute. Raymond Heslip. He got shifted to the drama department, I think it was. Doing odd jobs. Off-Broadway shows. It comes back a little. Gave him a by-line a few times. How I happen to remember his name. That's it. 'Raymond Heslip, Jr.' That's the way it was signed, I'm pretty sure. Come on, Jan."

"All right. Do I get to know where?"

"To the office," Phil Whitmore said. "To look at some pictures. Maybe read some clips. It's just around the corner."

The New York Chronicle Building was actually around two corners. After they had turned the first, and were walking south on Seventh Avenue, he touched her arm and directed her into the recessed doorway of an unlighted shop. They faced the sidewalk and, for more than a minute, he watched the people passing up and down. Many of them wore the sport shirts of tourists. Many of them were young and long-haired. Boys and girls, although often it was difficult to tell which, sometimes walked with arms around each other's waists. Janet, too, watched the people on the sidewalk. Then she turned and looked up at Phil Whitmore.

"Cloak-and-dagger?" Janet said.

He grinned at her.

"Not mine," he said. "Never wore a cloak in my life. Just, say, watching for a coincidence." He touched her arm again and they walked on down Seventh and turned the second corner.

The Chronicle Building was narrow and tall. All the windows were lighted. A man with a camera dangling on his chest hurried past them, and past the wide main entrance with a plaque with "The New York Chronicle" lettered on it, in old English script. The photographer went into the doorway beyond it, still hurrying.

"Got something for the final, probably," Phil said. "Or thinks he has. Thinks they'll make over and give him a by-line. Photographers!"

They followed the cameraman into the building. They went to an elevator marked "Editorial Only," and the operator said, "Evening, Mr. Whitmore. Keeps on being hot, don't it?" Whitmore said it sure as hell kept on being hot. The elevator stopped at the sixth floor and they went down a long corridor and, near its end, into a medium-size room with two desks, one larger than the other, and a window behind the larger. It was cool in the room.

"Window, even," Phil said. "Hope you're impressed, Jan. Doesn't open, of course." He motioned toward an armchair facing the desk and, after Janet sat on it, went to the chair behind the desk and took up a telephone. He said, "Whitmore. Copy, please," and cradled the phone. He put a cigarette in each corner of his wide mouth and lighted both and held one across the desk to Janet.

The cigarettes were half burned down when there was a quick double rap on the door. Phil said, "Yeah," and a tall blond boy of about eighteen came into the office. Unexpectedly, his hair was cut short. He said, "Good evening, Mr. Whitmore."

Phil said, " 'Lo, Jimmy. Picture morgue. Glossies of Dr. Paul Streeter and, if they've got them, of Raymond Heslip, Jr. He used to work here, tell Mr. Cunningham. And clips on both of them. Lot on Dr. Streeter, probably. Maybe nothing on Heslip. O.K.?"

Jimmy said, "Yes, sir," and went out.

"Nice kid, Jimmy Foster," Phil Whitmore said. "Wants to be a newspaperman. God knows why." He drew deeply on his cigarette. "Thinks being a copyboy is a way in. But he's going to Columbia this fall. School of Journalism. You have to have anyway a bachelor's to get a newspaper job nowadays. Years ago—before my time, even—you could start running copy and after a while get to write death notices. And maybe end up as a managing editor. Or, a lot more likely, a copyreader. Or what they call a librarian, which means a file clerk in the morgue, which the *Chronicle* likes us to call the Library."

He stubbed his cigarette out and shook another from the pack. "I smoke too damn much," he said, and held the open pack across the desk toward Janet. She shook her head, and Whitmore lighted his own.

"Now you have to have a degree to get started," he said, to the smoke he had just exhaled. He kept on looking at the swirling smoke.

After some seconds, Janet said, "A degree in journalism, Phil?"

It brought him back from wherever he had been. "Doesn't hurt," he said. "Teaches the techniques, anyway. Things any reasonably bright man can learn in a couple of months. Hell. A couple of weeks. Any man or any woman, I mean, of course."

"I'm not lib," Janet told him. "Not especially, anyhow. And after the techniques?"

"Huh?"

"What do you need then? To be what you are?"

"God knows. Luck, mostly. And no urge to make a fortune, of course. Oh, and—call it aptitude. Whatever I mean by that. Toughness, maybe. And curiosity. And an ability to put words together, I suppose. And, all right, having it the only thing you really want to do. People get out of it—get to be industrialists or certified public accountants or whatever—and keep coming up with that old bromide 'I used to be a newspaperman myself.' As if it were something to be proud of."

He dragged deeply on his cigarette, and shook his head again. Again, she waited some seconds. Then she said, "Well, isn't it, Philip?"

He ground his cigarette out. He smiled at her through the smoke between them.

"Years ago," he said, "I was a rewrite man on an afternoon. And, all right, I was damn good. We had six editions, starting with the home, which went to bed at ten-fifteen. Once or twice, when I was on the early shift, damn near all the front page was—"

A quick double rap on the office door interrupted him. He said, "Yeah?" and Jimmy Foster came in.

"Clips on Dr. Streeter are out, Mr. Whitmore. In the city room. Mr. Askew signed them out. Not much on Mr. Heslip, sir. But here are the pix."

The pix were two glossy photographs. He put them on the desk along with a brown, legal-size envelope, with "Heslip, Raymond, Jr." typed on it and, apparently, nothing in it. Whitmore looked at the two glossies and nodded his head slowly, and reached them across the desk to Janet. He opened the envelope.

A typed caption was pasted to the bottom of one of the photographs. It read, "Raymond Heslip, Jr." The photograph was, almost certainly, of the man who had told her his name was Coppell. On the back of the photograph, written in longhand, was Heslip's name again and "One Col."

She put the other eight-by-ten glossy beside the photograph of Heslip-Coppell. They looked a little alike but, on the whole, not a great deal alike. Paul Streeter had, for one thing, been a good deal the older when the photographs were taken. His brown hair had been turning gray; Heslip's hair was thick and there was no gray in it; there was youth in Heslip's face which had ebbed out of Streeter's. Janet looked across the desk at Phil Whitmore and shook her head.

He moved the photographs in front of him and looked at them. When he spoke, he spoke slowly.

"Pretty much the same jawline," he said. "Resemblance around the eyes. Not twins by a long shot, but—"

"Dr. Streeter is much older," Janet said. "His hair is showing gray. But then, so was Mr. Coppell's."

Phil said, "Read this," and put the single clip from Heslip's file envelope in front of her. The clip read:

Reporter Turns Thespian

Raymond Heslip, Jr., former member of the editorial staff of THE CHRONICLE, has a leading role in the off-Broadway production of "Papa Says No," a comedy by Archibald Framingham, now in its second week at the Brunswick Playhouse in East Eighty-sixth Street. He has had other parts in off-Broadway productions, notably as the elder brother in Edgar Norman's "Try, Try Again," produced last season at the Corner Craft's Theater in the Village. For several years, Mr. Heslip was a member of the editorial staff of this newspaper as a reporter and, later, as a member of the drama staff. He left THE CHRONICLE to join the staff of Brownell, Bernstein and Collins, the advertising agency.

"True to their own, newspapers are," Phil said. "When I cash in, I'll get a three quarters-column obit. Maybe a column. And Clay Carter, who reached millions to my thousands, got a short half. The *Chronicle* isn't partial to television. Rearguard action, I'm afraid. When I was a kid, newspapers used to put out extras when there was big spot news. Now we're just, as they say, in depth. And nobody cares much what candidate we endorse."

"All the same," Janet said, "you got on the enemies' list."

"Didn't make the top ten," Phil said. "Carter out-rated me by miles. Great disappointment to the M.E. Told me I must be slipping. And only half kidding, I'm afraid. To get back to the pix, Jan. It would be easy enough to add a touch of gray to the hair. Especially for an actor. And a little makeup could add the years."

"You're saying Mr. Heslip was just trying to confuse me? Why, Phil? It doesn't make sense."

"Wouldn't seem to," Phil Whitmore said. "Unless you saw Streeter somewhere he—or somebody—doesn't want you to remember. Some place—well—incriminating. Like a drag, say."

"I don't go to drags," Janet said. "I'm sure Dr. Streeter doesn't either. I've met his wife, Phil."

"All right. You can't remember where you *did* meet him? Because I think somebody's afraid you will. At your office, could it have been?"

She shook her head. She said, "I don't think so. It doesn't feel right. Of course, Clay had known him for years, apparently. I suppose he might have come in to see Clay sometime. When I was new there, maybe. Still mostly in the pool. But, no. It still doesn't feel right."

Phil said, "O.K." He turned the two photographs so that they again faced Janet. He said, "Look hard. Which one is the real mystery man?" His phrasing was more casual than his tone.

"Dr. Streeter, I'm pretty sure. Of course, Mr. Coppell's face is getting to look familiar. Or Mr. Heslip's, if that's who he is. Since I seem to be bumping into him, all at once. By coincidence, as you say."

Again, his gaze at her seemed for a moment oddly intense. But then he said, "Did I?" and shuffled the two glossies together and put the clip back in its envelope. He said, "We'll drop them off on our way. The

156

late city's going to bed and they'll have the boys hopping."

They left the office and went down the corridor and to a gray-haired man at a desk inside open double doors. Whitmore said, "Thanks, Ed," to the man at the desk and put the photographs and the envelope on the desk. The man said, "Any time, Phil," and they went back to the elevator. "Used to be a managing editor, Ed did," Whitmore said. "Chicago, I think it was. Could have been St. Louis."

They had to wait for a cab. The one they finally got was not air-conditioned. But it got them down to Waverly Place. Phil paid the cab off and followed Janet up the narrow stairs and into the almost cool apartment.

Inside, he did not reach toward her, as she had rather expected he would. Instead, he merely looked down at her, his gaze again thoughtful, intense. She looked up at him, smiling. One of his shoulders was still a little lower than the other. Which was a ridiculous thing to think.

"You can make us—" Janet said, and the telephone shrilled at them. She went to it and said, "Hullo?" After a moment, she again said, "Hullo?" her voice a little raised. Then she replaced the receiver and turned to Phil Whitmore.

"Nobody," she said. "Just that hollow sound and then the dial tone. When people hear the wrong voice and know they've dialed wrong, they ought at least to say they're sorry. Do you want to make us nightcaps, or shall—"

She stopped because he did not seem to be listening. Once more, his eyes seemed intent on her face. He shook his head slowly.

"Of course, it does happen that way," he said.

"People expect one voice and hear another and just hang up. Whoever called did hang up? I mean, you heard the sound?"

"Almost as soon as I spoke. Then the dial tone. Why, Phil? You don't think—Phil, it's something that happens all the time."

"It is also," he said, "a way of finding out whether anybody's home. Cognac, dear? Because I think I'm going to stick around a while. If you don't mind, of course."

"Have I ever minded?" Which was, of course, the wrong thing to say. It got the answer she had coming—"You're damn right you have." Then he said, "Things still where they used to be?" and when she said, "Yes, Philip," using his full name in defense, he went to get the "things"—small, stemmed liqueur glasses and the slight remains of a bottle of Remy Martin. The bottle, she thought, that I got all those months ago. The bottle from which we used to pour celebration drinks with nothing in particular to celebrate. No, with almost everything to celebrate.

He poured into the little glasses and they sat side by side on a sofa facing an empty fireplace. We used to have fires, she thought. A man used to bring logs from a cellar place in Ninth Street. Ridiculous little logs. Phil could always make them burn.

They clicked the little glasses together. Phil looked at her and smiled, and then looked at the empty fireplace as if, she thought, he too were seeing long-ago fires flickering in it. But when he spoke, it was not of long-extinguished fires. (Or not really extinguished fires?) He spoke very slowly.

"Somebody thinks you'll remember," he said. "Doesn't want you to remember. Doesn't want you to remember and—and tell anybody. Anybody who could,

I suppose, do something about whatever it is. Who could, say, spread it around. Somebody like Clay Carter. Or, come to that, somebody like me, I suppose. Of course, Clay's dead."

He looked at her, then. She looked back at him. "Yes," Janet said, "Clay's dead, Phil." She kept her voice very steady. It wasn't as hard to keep it so as it had been two days ago.

"*Killed* dead," Phil said. "Did you tell him about this feeling you'd seen Streeter somewhere before?"

"Probably. I'm not really sure."

"And that you couldn't remember where?"

"If I mentioned it at all, yes, I must have. What are you getting at, Phil?"

He shrugged his shoulders and said, "I don't know. Nothing, probably."

"You think somebody killed Clay because—well, because he knew something I hadn't told him? That's—"

"I know it doesn't make much sense, Jan. But if somebody thought you'd remembered. Or almost certainly would remember. Somebody who was thinking ahead. A long way ahead. Taking care of things that just might happen. Oh, it's all pretty muzzy. I don't deny that."

"And vague, Phil. I know I didn't see Dr. Streeter —well, shoot somebody. Or break open a safe. And— look—if somebody thought I know, or might remember, something, why not just kill me? Why—oh, murder around the bush? It's—it's all fantasy, Phil."

Phil said it sounded like it. And that she would, he supposed, be at the top of any killer's list.

"And," Janet said, "if there's anything to this fantasy of yours, you'd be next on the list, wouldn't you? If I remembered something dangerous to somebody,

I might tell you, mightn't I? And you could what you call spread it around as well as anybody."

"You know, Janet dear, I'd just happened to think of that," Phil said. And he smiled widely at her, and again they clicked the little glasses together. But the glasses were almost empty.

It was a little after midnight when Philip Whitmore stood outside the apartment and listened for, and heard, the two clicking sounds which meant that Janet had put the bolting lock on and lodged the chain in its slot. He had made her promise that she would; had told her he would wait outside to make sure she did. And before he left the apartment, he had made certain that the bedroom windows, which opened on the extended kitchen roof of the ground-floor apartment, from which an iron fire ladder reached down to the fenced "garden"—in which only a rather discouraged tree grew—were securely fastened. Not that locked windows would stop anybody of determination.

His precautions had, he knew, increased the uneasiness growing in both of them. Uneasiness, he thought, which I aroused, which I stirred up for no tangible reason, none I could put a finger on. It was seeing Heslip at the bar which triggered me, he thought. Probably he goes there every night for his beer. A good many *Chronicle* people do. Or former *Chronicle* people. It's melodramatic to think he may have followed us there. It's cloak-and-dagger, as she said.

In the bedroom, he had looked only briefly at the wide bed—the once-familiar bed. But there was a sharp picture of it in his mind as he went reluctantly down the stairs, having done all he could to safeguard Janet Osborne against a threat which probably did not exist. Well, not all I could have done. I could have alerted the police. I could have stayed in the apartment. Slept on the sofa in the living room, if that had been the way she wanted it.

It wouldn't have been. I know that and I'm sure she knows that. But I had frightened her. To that degree weakened her. I don't want it that way. If we begin over—and now I think we will begin over—it will be as it used to be, our choice free and shared freely, with no other need than our need for each other.

He went down the stairs. The block of Waverly Place between the Square and Sixth Avenue had cars parked on either side, but no cars moving in it. It was not a block which promised cabs. He walked toward Sixth.

When he was midway of the block, and in a section where no cars lined the curb—in unexpected obedience to a sign which read "No Parking at Any Time" —he heard a car engine start up behind him; start up racing. A taxi, by some miracle? He stood near the curb and looked toward the Square.

Not a miracle cab, with a lighted sign on its roof. A car, pulling away from the curb on the downtown side of the street. So—Sixth Avenue, as he had supposed. He began to walk on toward Sixth. From the raising pitch of the car engine behind him, somebody was in one hell of a hurry, Phil thought. He glanced back. It was a big car and it was certainly in a—

He jumped back as the car swerved toward him. Some crazy drunk. Some—

The car, heading toward him, did not swerve back into the roadway. It hit the curb and bounced over it. Phil threw himself down and away from the charging car. He was not quite quick enough. The right front fender brushed brutally against his hip and he was sliding on the sidewalk, the pavement tearing at his jacket, abrading his extended, protective hands. A hedge of bushes stopped him. The bushes scratched his face. Lying stretched out on the sidewalk, he heard the car which had struck him receding through Waverly Place. He rolled over and was in time to see a car turning right into Sixth Avenue. At least, the drunken fool knew Sixth was one way, uptown. He could still tell green from red. The crazy son of—

I wonder if I can get up, Phil thought. I wonder if I'm getting blood all over somebody's ornamental hedge? Lucky I was knocked into it, instead of up against a stone step.

His left hip hurt. Broken? Only one way to find out.

Philip Whitmore pushed himself to a sitting position. The left leg seemed to work all right; not without hurting, but subject to the mind's orders. He used the hedge to help him and pulled himself to his feet. He could stand on them.

A handkerchief patted gently on his face came away only slightly reddened. He could use his feet to walk on, experimentally at first, then with more confidence. He would have a hell of a bruise on his hip. His jacket would never be the same again. His bruised hands probably would fumble on his typewriter for a few days. I'm lucky not to be more banged up, Phil thought, as he walked on toward Sixth. Hell, I'm lucky to be alive. Not the fault of that son of a bitch. He came right at me. He could almost have been aiming—

He almost stopped.

He *was* aiming at me, Phil thought. He was no more a reckless drunk than I am.

Jan is maybe a dangerous girl to know.

11

MY JOB IS TO EVALUATE EVIDENCE, Bernie Simmons had
thought, still sitting at his desk at a quarter of six;
to decide what charge, if any, the evidence justifies.
Which is fine if there is evidence to evaluate. What
the hell is Johnny Stein doing; what are the dozens
of detectives working on the case doing? And, come
to that, what have I been doing all this afternoon except shuffling routine papers concerned with other matters? Not, God knows, that there has been a lack of
other matters.

Mary Leffing had gone at five, as she had been supposed to. She had stood in the doorway between the
offices for a minute or two and watched him shuffle
papers. She had said, "It's five o'clock, Mr. Simmons,"
and he had turned and looked at her. She had shaken
her head in reproach.

"Go home, Mary," Bernie said. She shook her head
again.

"A few things to clear up," Bernie told her. "Then

I'll go too." She's protective, he thought. "Plug into my phone before you go," he said. "I'll be around for half an hour or so."

"Well," Mary Leffing said, with doubt in her voice. But she went. The telephone on his desk tinkled once as she plugged through. He heard her office door close and the click of her receding heels in the corridor. He read that the jury, *People of the State of New York* v. *Albert Smirnoff,* was still out after four hours and that it had requested, and received, transcript of the testimony of Louise Sheridan, witness for the State. Juries niggle. It was open-and-shut, and ADA Roy Watkins hadn't bungled it. All right, there have to be juries.

I promised her I'd make it by seven. I've got to go up to the apartment and shower and change. If I leave now, I can just make it. If I can find a cab. Of which, the chance is about one in a hundred. So—

He pushed his chair back from the desk. The time was five-forty-eight. The telephone rang, and Assistant District Attorney Bernard Simmons sat down again, and said "Simmons" into the receiver.

"Caught you," John Stein said. "They did meet for lunch, Bernie. Like I thought they would."

"Fine," Simmons said. "Who met—oh, sure, Johnny. Willis and Mrs. Carter. And?"

"At the Spanish Pavilion. For damn near two hours. And went back to her apartment for another couple of hours. Plenty of time, I'd say."

"And to spare, John. Then?"

"He went back to his office. Still there, Mahoney says. Detective Francis Mahoney. He's taken over. So much for the producer he was supposed to be meeting. Producer, one Grace Carter. Production, one hell of a lot of money, and a wad of stock in IBC. Well, Counselor?"

"No, Johnny. Motive. I'll buy that. But not enough by miles. You know that, Johnny."

"Just filling you in," Stein said. "Motive. Knew where Carter lived. Knew Carter always lugged the TV set around. Probably knew Carter's car when he saw it parked in front of Carter's house. Used to be a technical man, few years back. Obviously knows how to short out a TV receiver. Could have found out that Carter was going up to Mt. Kisco and expected to be back late Saturday night and gone up there and waited around and—"

"Did he? I mean, call Johnson and check Carter?"

"Somebody did, Johnson says. A woman, he thinks. Or maybe a man with a light voice. No, Bernie. No name. Could have been Mrs. Carter. Setting it up for her playmate."

"Yes. And it could have been anybody. Carter had a dinner date the night he was killed. Find out yet with whom?"

"Yes. With Peter Graham, president of the network. According to Graham, Carter called him up Saturday night and said they ought to get together. Didn't say about what, Graham says, but he thinks probably about this Latham, who'd taken over as Saturday night newscaster. Graham says he'd been expecting Carter to blow up about Latham. So he arranged to have dinner with Carter Sunday night. Then Carter didn't show up, of course. Graham waited and waited and finally called Carter's house, he says, when the police were there. So he learned of Carter's death from Johnson before it was broadcast. And, he says, he was just guessing as to why Carter wanted to see him in such a hurry."

"There was a hurry?"

"Seemed to be, Graham said."

"Carter didn't say it was about this man Latham?

That's just Graham's assumption?"

"Yes. A side issue, obviously. There are always side issues, Counselor."

"Don't I know, Captain. Speaking of that, did the cat come back? Or don't you know?"

"The cat came back in about half an hour. Ate his food, Johnson says. Then went up to Carter's bed to —well, to wait, I guess. Did you know cats were like that, Bernie?"

Bernie said he didn't know much about cats. He said he had a date with somebody who did and he'd ask her about it. He was told to give Miss Curran John Stein's best.

Bernie looked at his watch. Already it was a few minutes after six. Bernie said, "If that's all, John? It's still no on Willis. Not yet, anyway."

"Just keeping you up to date," Stein said. "Oh, there's one more side issue. Way off side. Know anything about a firm of private investigators called Conover and—hold it a minute—Conover and Comfortobelli?"

He was asked to spell it. He spelled it. Bernie said, "Jesus!" and Stein said he couldn't agree more. Bernie said, "Why, John?"

"Query from the State Police. Seems a car registered to Conover and so forth ran into a truck while a trooper was chasing it for speeding outside Mt. Kisco. Banged the car up a bit and banged the driver up a bit. Man named Pfeiffer—Arnold Pfeiffer. Licensed private investigator. Had a thirty-eight in the car. License for that, too. Also, a briefcase with a lot of new hundred-dollar bills in it."

"Refugee from Watergate, John?"

"Payoff in a jewel recovery, Pfeiffer says. Implies, anyway. To the trooper who cleaned up after him. Man named Turner, the trooper is. Says he had pulled off into a side road to—well, lie in wait, I suppose. There not being any billboard handy to hide behind. Just taking time out for a breather and a cigarette, be my guess. Anyway, this Pfeiffer went by on the main road and Turner took off after him. Caught him when a truck nosed out into the main road to be run into. You people know anything about Conover and so forth, Bernie?"

"I don't. I'll check it tomorrow, to keep the State cops happy, if you like. Nothing to do with us that I can see. Wait a minute. Around Mt. Kisco, you say?"

"Yeah, way we get it. Conover and whatnot doesn't seem to be listed in the telephone book. There's a ConCom Investigations. Could be the same thing, I suppose. Easier than Comfortobelli."

"As what isn't," Bernie said. "Reason I asked about Mt. Kisco, John—Carter was up that way Saturday. Day before he was killed. So was I. At Paul Streeter's new place. Happen to know the name of this road the trooper was lurking in?"

"Lurking is pejorative, Counselor. Accurate, but pejorative. Maybe I've got it here somewhere. Seems to me—yeah. Something called Pinetree Lane. Hey!"

"Yes, Johnny. The road Streeter lives on. Dead-ends a mile or so beyond the Streeter house. Only, this man Pfeiffer wasn't on it, was he?"

"No. On the main road. Going seventy, the trooper says. Summoned him for that, the trooper said. Thirty over the limit. Supposed to show up before a J.P. Friday to pay his fine, this private investigator is."

Bernie Simmons said, "Mmmm," and then, after a moment, said it again.

"Maybe," he said then, "your boys better check out this Conover and whatnot, Captain. Tomorrow, maybe.

And perhaps have a little talk with this trooper, whatever his name is. Think so, John?"

"His name's Turner," Stein said. "Yes, I guess maybe we'd better. Not that Willis isn't our man, Bernie."

"Yes," Simmons said. "Simpler that way. And ten to one it's the right way. However—"

"Good night, Counselor. And give Miss Curran my best."

There was a cab loitering through the hot murk outside the Criminal Courts Building. It was only ten minutes after seven when Bernard Simmons pushed the bell button outside the door marked 5J and heard the loud clatter of the bell inside—and heard the quick tapping of heels coming toward the door. She always sounds as if she were running, Bernie thought. It's fine she hurries so to let me in. Even when I'm a little late. "Hi, lady. Hi, darling." He held her close for a moment. He released her and held her away from him, his hands on her shoulders, and looked down at her for some seconds.

"I'll make us drinks," Bernie said. "You look as if you could do with a drink."

"You read me," Nora said. "Loud and clear, you read me. The glasses are frozen."

He mixed martinis and poured them into the frozen glasses. They clicked glasses and Nora drank from hers quickly, which was not like her. She put her glass down on the table in front of the sofa and looked at the opposite wall, and said, "You know something's going to happen and still, when it does, you're not ready for it." She turned and looked at him. Her smile wasn't a very good smile.

"We've been swallowed," Nora Curran said. "Swallowed whole. We heard about it today. All the heads heard about it and it trickled down. Passed down, in my case."

"Materson's?"

"Materson's. In one gulp, apparently. Oh, exchange of stock. Something like that. Or purchase of the majority interest. Ted wasn't too clear about that. He was one of those called in to meet the new executive vice-president, they call him."

Ted, Bernie knew, was Theodore Baker, senior editor of the trade books division of Materson & Brothers. Nora was an assistant editor under Baker.

"Trade books," Nora said. "Educational. Medical. Even the juvenile editor. All the departments. Called in to meet the new coordinator. Executive vice-president and coordinator. That's what they're going to call him. You'll never believe his real name, Bernie."

He said, "Try me, dear," and watched her lift her cocktail glass and almost empty it. Which wasn't in the least like Nora Curran, who is a sipper. Bernie sipped from his own glass.

"Jeremiah Jenkins," Nora said. "Nobody's really named Jeremiah. Jeremiah Jenkins. 'But almost everybody calls me J.J.' "

"I'll bet," Bernie said, and shook a cigarette loose in a pack and held it out to her. He held a lighter flame out, too. She drew deeply on the cigarette. He lighted a cigarette of his own.

"Everything's going to be the same," Nora said. "No change in policy. Mr. Eaton stays as editor-in-chief, of course. With an absolutely free hand. They may put in a few assistant editors, just to keep in touch with things. Only temporarily, of course. And you know what Ted says about that, dear?"

"I can guess," Bernie said. " 'In a pig's eye,' Baker says. Or words to that effect."

"Clairvoyant," Nora said. "That's what's going to make us fresh drinks. A clairvoyant. 'In a pig's eye' was just what Ted said. Where does that phrase come from, Bernie? I've heard it all my life, but where does it come from?"

"I haven't the foggiest," Bernie said and finished his drink and carried their emptied glasses back to the refrigerator and got freshly chilled glasses out of it. This time he made the martinis with only an ounce of gin. If they were going to drink at this rate—and go out to dinner. She's had a jolt, he thought, as he carried the renewed drinks back to the table in front of the sofa.

Nora looked at the diminished liquid in her glass and smiled at it. She turned to Bernie and smiled at him and nodded her head. She said, "All right, darling. I was shook up."

"Darling" is a word Nora Curran does not use without consideration, and Bernie was pleased to hear her use it now. "This 'they,' " he said. "Bartwell Industries, as you expected? As all the rumors had it?"

"No," she said. "That's the funny thing about it. One of the funny things. Something I never heard of before. Something called Consolidated Communications. Sounds—oh, pompous, doesn't it? Did you ever hear of a Consolidated Communication, Bernie?"

"Yes," Bernie Simmons said. "I've heard of it, Nora." It was his turn to look at the wall across the room from them. "Maybe not enough of it," he said, more to himself than to her. She waited, but he did not go on with that. He said, "Where will you stand at Materson now? Or don't you know?"

"For a while," she said, "I suppose I'll be an assistant assistant editor. Until Ted moves on, as I'm pretty sure he will. And knows he can. Taking three or four of his writers with him, probably. Which will serve this—this gobbling whale—right. And I'll be shaken out. Where do we go to dinner? Some simple, quiet place, the way I feel."

Armand's was near. They could walk to Armand's. It would be quiet. It was "one of those little places almost nobody knows about."

As they walked into the small restaurant, Bernie said, "Damn it to hell," which was the only suitable thing to say.

"I forgot," Nora said. "That man on the *Chronicle* discovered it Monday."

There is nothing that takes the quiet out of a side street in Manhattan like "discovery" by the "Where to Dine" columnist of the New York *Chronicle*.

"An automat," Bernie said. "Or maybe the Plaza."

But Armand himself, thin and dark-haired, wearing a dark suit and a very thick blue tie, came up to them with a smile almost broader than his necktie, and said, "Mr. *Simmons*," in the tone of one who has found Dr. Livingstone in a jungle. "And *madame*. Your table is ready, m'sieu-madame." It sometimes pays to be an assistant district attorney, County of New York. And to have hair so surprisingly red that nobody can forget it.

The table against the wall was not really ready. A bus was taking used dishes off it. They had to wait while he put on a fresh tablecloth. It was not either secluded or quiet; neither condition was anywhere in the small restaurant crowded by a paragraph in the *Chronicle*.

"Busy tonight," Bernie said, and Armand said "M'sieu!" as an exclamation. He calmed himself, and said, "A cocktail first, m'sieu-madame?" They ordered drinks. The busboy put silver on the table, said,

"M'sieu-madame," on a note of triumph and went away.

"You told me once you used to have a cat," Bernie said and was answered by a look of astonishment and then by, "Yes, dear. An all-black cat named Diogenes. I was eleven or twelve and I'd just heard of Diogenes. And why on earth?"

"Somebody asked me about cats," Bernie said. "I said I knew somebody who maybe knew about them and that I'd—"

She said, "Oh," relief in her voice, reassured that his wits had not left him. "What about cats?"

"Whether they are attached to people, or just to places. Clayton Carter had a cat. A long Siamese named Mao. Mao's been looking all over for Carter. Crouching on Carter's bed. Not eating. Is that like cats?"

"I've only known three cats, dear. One when I was very small. A kitten, who died of something. And Dio —it boiled down to that, of course"—she pronounced it Dye-oh—"and Lucinda, she was a longhair, sometime in my 'teens. None of them was like anybody except himself. Oh, they all had four feet. And tails. People have two feet. What's 'like' people, Bernie?"

"Monkeys. Once in a million, saints. All right. Take Diogenes, for one."

"I was about twelve. Dio was my cat. He was all black—not a white hair on him. He didn't like people much. Oh, he was polite to them, in a detached sort of way. But he loved me. I think he did. All right, I know he did. I was his human, and—"

A waiter brought their drinks. Bernie said, "Thank you."

"That summer," Nora said, "my parents decided I ought to go to a camp. Thought I ought to know more girls my own age. I hated it at camp, Bernie.

They made us do exercises before breakfast. And run races. And—well, I didn't want to be there. But I had to stay and finally I got mad and won one of those damn races."

She was looking toward him, but she did not seem to see him.

"Look back in hatred," Bernie said. "About Dio, Nora child?"

"He stopped eating. They didn't tell me. They should have told me, shouldn't they? For more than a week he wouldn't eat. And then they let him out and he didn't come back. I never saw him again, although when I did get back I went all over the neighborhood calling him. We lived up in Westchester then, and Dorothy was just—just toddling around. I kept thinking he would hear me and know things were all right again. But I never found him. I hoped he had found somebody else, but I'm afraid—"

She stopped talking and lifted her glass. She did not reach it out to click with his. I'm a damn fool, Bernie Simmons thought. What the hell do I really care about a cat named Mao? Enough about cats; too much about cats, since a long-lost cat still worried her.

A waiter came and, yes, they would order—*canard l'orange flambé*. And yes, cocktails while they waited. The drinks came quickly; customers (those who had waited for tables not "reserved") had thinned at the bar. This time she held her glass toward his. They clicked glasses.

"What happens to Mr. Carter's cat?" Nora said.

Enough of cats, Bernie thought. How did we ever get on cats? Bernie said he didn't know what would happen to the cat named Mao. He said that he supposed Carter's man would feed Mao, if Mao wanted to eat, as long as Carter's man stayed on in the house on

Riverside. And that would be up to Mrs. Carter. He spoke in the tone of one ending a subject.

Nora said, "Oh." Then she said, "Does this Mrs. Carter like cats?"

Bernie didn't know how Grace Carter felt about cats. They sipped. Duckling came and was flamed at the table. Although Armand's was moderately air-conditioned, it was a hot night to sit by a bonfire. But the duck was good. Bernie ate with avidity, a little to his surprise. Nora ate with noticeably less interest. She only sipped at the wine he had ordered, although it was good enough wine. He looked across the table at her.

"It's fine food," Nora said. "I'm just not very hungry, is all. And all this noise."

There was noise in the small restaurant. Bernie hadn't thought there was all that much noise. They would have been better off in her apartment. He could have got sandwiches from the delicatessen on Third Avenue. And he shouldn't have brought up cats. Not that it was at all about cats.

They had coffee and said little while they drank it. Outside, a taxicab was discharging a couple who had, rather too obviously, been to an extended cocktail party. Nora started to walk on, but Bernie touched her arm and she stopped. She said, "All right. It's silly, but all right." Inside the cab he put an arm around her. After a second she relaxed against him.

"Go through the park," Bernie told the cabbie, who said, "O.K., Mac." Nora Curran said nothing. She closed her eyes.

The cab went up Madison and through Fifty-ninth and into Central Park, and neither of them said anything. The air which came through the open windows was warm air, but it was moving air. In the park, it even tasted a little like air. She took hold of the hand of the arm which circled her and held onto it. After a time, she said, "I'm sorry. I spoiled it for us. I'm sorry, darling."

He said she had nothing to be sorry about. She tightened her hand on his. She opened her eyes and looked at him. "Sometimes," she said, "things just seem to fall apart. Partly, it was remembering being a little girl. And Dorothy's being not much more than a baby."

We keep circling back to Dorothy, Bernie thought. Dorothy keeps on coming between us. He said, "Things will come back together, Nora. It's a habit things have."

The pressure of her hand in his increased momentarily, which was, in a way, an answer. They were nearing the upper end of Central Park when she answered him in words.

"Oh," she said, "they'll come back together. They are coming back together, Bernie. It was dear of you to think of the park. I used to walk in the park a few years ago. Before people got afraid to. Did you ever walk in the park, Bernie?"

"From Columbus Circle up to the museum," he said. "I can't say I ever ran around the reservoir."

"Do you suppose people still do?" she said. But it was not really a question, waiting for an answer. Anyway, Bernie didn't know whether men still ran earnestly on the footpath around the reservoir in Central Park. They were rounding toward the west side of the park before he spoke again. Then he said, "Dorothy's all right?"

He knew that Dorothy, who had once danced to no music audible to other ears, who had once tried to throw herself out of a third-floor window, was no longer in the mental hospital. He knew that Nora's younger sister was living in a small apartment in the building

Nora lived in, and that a companion was living there with her, and that Nora was paying for the apartment and for the companion. And that Nora was now afraid that she was going to lose her job. And that Nora would not let him help. Once she had told him that, when she was a little girl, she had said so often, "I do it my seps," that the phrase had become a family saying, and one to be gently laughed at. And he knew that Dorothy, and the depth of Nora's feeling of responsibility for Dorothy, still was a wall between them. Not a tangible wall. Not a wall impenetrable. Not, to him, a wall which made sense. But it was not to him that it had to make sense.

"She's all right," Nora said. "She's coming along fine, Dr. Werkes says. But I'm still all she has, dear. All she has to hold onto. She—she's beginning to talk about getting a job. Trying to get a job. And she met a boy and let him take her to lunch. And she liked him, I think. Anyway, she said she did. But he wanted to take her to dinner and she told him no—told him she already had a date. But she didn't. She—she's still afraid of night, Bernie. It was night, you know, when she tried—tried—"

He kissed her, to stop her speech. Then for other reasons. They were holding hard to each other when the cab went out of the park and down Fifth. They drew a little apart when the hacker said, "Where now, Mac?"

Bernie told him where now, and they turned left into Fifty-second Street. The light stopped them at Madison.

"Speaking of Saturday at the Streeters'," Bernie said. "Not that we were. You talked some with Janet Osborne, Carter's friend?"

"Yes, Bernie."

"About what, do you remember?"

"Bartwell Industries taking over Materson. That they were trying to take over IBC too. That Bartwell is an octopus. International octopus. She's a nice person. Easy to talk to. Why?"

"Because Carter's dead. She say anything about having seen Streeter somewhere before? And not being able to remember where?"

"Or when. Yes, dear."

The light changed. A red light stopped them again at Park.

"Did anybody overhear her say that, do you think?"

She had drawn away a little, far enough so that she could look at him.

"Dear," Nora said, "we were all over the terrace. Mr. Carter was sitting next to her, I think. You and Dr. Streeter were sort of—oh, walking around. We weren't speaking loudly, but I suppose anybody could have heard us if they wanted to listen. Including the maid, I suppose."

"Dr. Streeter? Mrs. Streeter?"

"Most of the time he was at the end of the terrace, making drinks. I think he was. She, I think, was sitting on the other side of the terrace, more or less facing us."

The light changed. The cab crossed Park and made it to the red light at Lexington. Nora looked at the red-haired man and raised her eyebrows, but he only tightened his arm around her. She relaxed against him. They crossed Lexington and Third and the cabbie said, "Here we are, Mac."

They rode up to Apartment 5J and she let them into it. They had left a lamp turned on. She flicked up a switch and other lights went on. He flicked the switch down again. They sat together on the sofa, beside which the lamp glowed softly. For a time neither spoke.

"Look," Bernie said, his voice only a murmur. "We love each other. Agreed?"

She nodded her head against his shoulder.

"So," Bernie said, "we ought to marry each other. It's only logical. Like the horse and carriage."

She did not stiffen in his arm, but her head moved against his shoulder. The movement was one of negation. She did not speak.

"You're afraid you'll lose your job," he said. "Won't be able to go on taking care of Dorothy. Maybe you're right. But I have a job. Together, we could take care of her. She's kept us apart too damn long, Nora."

She moved enough to smile up at him.

"Apart?" Nora Curran said. "I don't know that that's quite the word, Bernie."

He kissed her. His hands tightened on her. But, gently, she drew away a little.

"About Dorothy," she said. "It isn't just the money. Oh, once that was a lot of it. That I was responsible for her; that I couldn't push that responsibility off on anyone. Even part of it. Even on you. I don't feel so much that way now. Oh, some, but not so much. It's—I don't really know how to put it, dear. If we get married—not just lovers, but tied together. I don't mean just legally. Or at all legally, really. But just—oh, all of each of us to the other. That's the way I'd want it, anyway. I think you do, too; think that's why you keep talking about marriage. We'd—well, want all of each other. Yes?"

"Yes."

"There wouldn't be room for anybody else, I mean. Oh, we wouldn't hide ourselves—our*self*, really—in a cave. You'd go on trying people; I'd go on editing—if I had a job. We'd see people. But they'd be—oh, outside people. Tangential. Am I being silly, darling? Sappy, maybe?"

"No, Nora. Not that I—"

She did not wait for him to finish. "Dorothy would be one of the outsiders. There'd be a wall around us, keeping her out. She can't stand that, Bernie. Not yet, anyway. She'd just slip back. Slip away. She'd feel alone. She's not strong enough to be alone. She's getting stronger, I think. When she can go it alone, I'd love to have ourselves become ourself. But, I can't wall her off. And, it would be walling her off. If I felt I had—well, it wouldn't be right with us, either. Don't you see that, darling?"

" 'Had we but world enough and time,' " Bernard Simmons said and drew her back against him.

After a little while, Nora said, "I take it you don't hold out for marriage, darling."

Bernie said he didn't hold out for marriage.

They got up from the sofa, his arm still around her, and walked down the living room.

12

THE ANGRY JANGLING of a bell wakened Bernard Simmons. Damn doorbell, he thought. Have to get it muffled somehow. It's all right, darling. I'll get it. I—he reached to the side of the bed to touch and reassure her. There wasn't anybody on the other side of the bed. He wasn't in bed in Apartment 5J in East Fifty-second Street. He was in his own bed in his own flat in East Sixty-sixth. The bell jangled again. Bernard Simmons reached for the telephone beside his bed and said a sleepy, surly "Yeah?" into it.

"Phil Whitmore, Bernie. You sound as if I'd waked you up. It's almost eight. Time to be up and doing."

"You sure as hell waked me up."

"Sorry. Couple of things you ought to know. This Coppell guy Jan thought was Streeter isn't. Also, he isn't named Coppell. You tracking now, Bernie? Janet Osborne. Man she met in Waverly Place and confused with Dr. Streeter. Thought it solved what had been troubling her and—"

"All right, I'm tracking. You don't need to spell it out, Seer. Not Streeter. Also not Coppell. Who?"

"Man named Heslip. Used to work on the *Chronicle*. Drama department. On the stage for a while. Looks a little like Streeter maybe looked a few years back. Oh, and somebody tried to kill me last night. Run a car over me."

Bernie said, "What the hell?"

Phil Whitmore told him about the night before—about Heslip's appearance at the bar, about the photographs he and Janet had looked at in his office at the *Chronicle*.

At intervals, as he listened, Bernie said, "Mmmm." Once he said, "You think Heslip followed you and Miss Osborne to Larry's restaurant?" Phil Whitmore said he didn't know; said he had wondered. Bernie said, "Mmmm." He said, "Tell me about this car that tried to run you down."

Whitmore told him about the car which had charged the curb in Waverly Place.

"You told the police?"

"No point to it. I don't know the make of the car. Or the license number. It just grazed me, so it wouldn't have a bashed-up fender. And it maybe was just a drunk at the wheel. What could the cops do, Counselor? File and forget? Or just forget to file?"

Bernie said, "All right. And I hope Miss Osborne's all right too."

She was. Whitmore had just telephoned her. "Waked her up, too." Janet was fine. Whitmore was going to pick her up at nine-fifteen or so and take her to work. "In a cab. Cab a friend of mine drives."

Bernie said, "O.K. Maybe it's a good idea." Then he said, "By the way," and Phil Whitmore said, "Yeah?"

"You sent for clips on Paul Streeter and they were out. In the city room. Why would that be, Phil?"

"Background material on him, I suppose. To stretch out some story about him. Unless he suddenly popped off, of course. Could be for an obit. Although, since he's fairly well known, we'd have that in type, probably."

"O.K., Phil."

"Sorry I waked you up. Thought I ought to fill you in."

"It's all right," Bernie said. "I'm glad you did, Seer. Don't get run over by an automobile."

Bernie Simmons showered and shaved and made himself a soft-boiled egg and coffee. Must have got in about three, he thought. What she's got about our marriage is just a block. People aren't all that responsible for other people. Hell, she's not her sister's keeper. Maybe I ought to call up and tell her that. Or just tell her she's wonderful.

He did not. Instead, he had a third cup of coffee and two cigarettes instead of one. Five hours' sleep isn't enough hours' sleep. I ought to feel bushed. Instead, I feel swell.

It was going to be another smothering day. He walked to Lexington and bought a copy of the *Chronicle* and flagged down a cab. He opened the *Chronicle*. The President had vetoed a bill which would have added some millions of Federal funds to the amount of aid available for urban public transport. The Senate was expected to override. The House was expected to sustain. The President, in his message, chided Congress for fiscal irresponsibility. He had signed a supplementary appropriations bill alloting a billion and a half dollars (and seventy-four cents) to the Defense Department for research on, and preliminary construction of, a supersonic bomber which would eventually replace the soon-to-be-obsolescent B52. He had chided Congress on that one, too. The appropriation was totally inadequate. The Congress was imperiling national security. It had been listening to dissident elements.

Below the fold on the front page was a single-column head:

FCC NOMINATION
ASTOUNDS CAPITOL
**Liberal Professor Named
To Fill Vacancy**

The text, under a Washington dateline, read:

The President today nominated Dr. Paul Streeter, professor of public communications at Dyckman University, to the chairmanship of the Federal Communications Commission, a post left vacant by the recent retirement of Alexander Hopkins. The nomination, which is expected to be promptly confirmed by the Senate, astounded many Washington observers, since Dr. Streeter has long been known as a supporter of liberal causes and, three years ago, vigorously defended television news coverage before a House committee hearing.

Dr. Streeter's nomination, when confirmed, can be expected to result in a much more favorable FCC attitude toward broadcast journalism, which has long been a target of criticism by Administration spokesmen. A majority of the commission, insured by Dr. Streeter's membership, may save the licenses of several "liberal" stations which have come under Administration attack for alleged violation of the fairness doctrine.

It had been widely assumed here that the President would take advantage of Mr. Hopkins's retirement, which is to take effect on September 1, to appoint as FCC chairman a man more in line

183

with Administration thinking. The name of Hiram Whiteside, former Congressman from Texas, who was defeated in the last election, has been widely mentioned in Washington circles as Mr. Hopkins's likely successor. Mr. Whiteside, in his unsuccessful campaign, urged repeal of the income tax and the substitution of a sales tax on all commodities.

Mr. Hopkins, although his record is by no means as "liberal" as that of Dr. Streeter, has recently voted against the Administration on several licensing proposals, swinging the seven-man commission toward a position supported by most broadcasting interests.

Dr. Streeter's presence as FCC head is expected to lessen Administration threats to broadcast journalism.

Among the stations likely to be affected is WIBC, the New York outlet wholly owned by the Independent Broadcasting Company. The license under which WIBC operates comes up for renewal in mid-August. The renewal is expected to be challenged by at least one corporation, reputedly one which now operates a number of radio stations throughout the country, many of which are felt by some to be advocating programs similar to those espoused by the John Birch Society.

Another organization which has been expected to challenge renewal of WIBC's license is reputedly affiliated with the Veterans of Foreign Wars, before (Continued on Page 48, Col. 1)

Bernie did not turn to page 48; the New York *Chronicle* is bulky to rearrange in a bouncing taxicab. He did look at the one-column cut which accompanied the story on page 1. It was sharp and clear, an excellent likeness of Paul Streeter, Ph.D., Edward R. Murrow Professor of Public Communications at Dyckman University. It had, Bernie thought, been made from a very recent photograph of Paul. Paul probably would have to get a leave of absence from Dyckman. Have to commute between the house near Mt. Kisco and Washington. Wouldn't get as much time for tennis, probably.

Bernie paid off the cab and rode up to his office, carrying the *Chronicle*. He was early; Mary Leffing, by whom one could set clocks, was not yet at her desk. Bernie turned to page 48, column 1.

(Continued from Page 1)
which the Chief Executive recently made a vigorous speech on national security.

Dr. Streeter has been at Dyckman University for more than five years, assuming the Edward R. Murrow chair, named in honor of the late correspondent and crusading reporter of the Columbia Broadcasting System, three years ago.

Born in California, Dr. Streeter was educated in the San Francisco public schools and received his B.A. from Berkeley. He earned his master's at the same institution. He received his doctorate at Yale. He was an associate professor at New Haven before joining the faculty at Dyckman.

He was a vigorous opponent of the Vietnam war, a stand which reputedly prevented his appointment as a communications consultant in the Johnson administration. He is known to have been under active consideration for such a post prior to the publication of his "The Domino Theory: Examination of a Subterfuge."

He is the author of several other books, including "The First Amendment: A Bulwark of Freedom," which many political scientists consider a definitive work.

Whatever that may mean, Bernie thought. He put

the paper aside and said, "Morning, Mary," through the open door to the adjacent office.

Mary Leffing said, "Good morning, Mr. Simmons," and closed the door. Then she opened it again and filled his In basket with papers.

He began the morning's tedious journey through yesterday's events, approving them with initials—his under those of his bureau chief, further under the vigorous B.H. of the District Attorney, County of New York. Judge Philpotts had accepted the second-degree plea of Zirkin's client; had withheld sentence pending a probation report. The Fraud Bureau had no investigation pending of Consolidated Communications, which was listed on the American Stock Exchange, yesterday's closing 31¼. Assistant District Attorney Hiram—

The telephone rang on his desk. "Captain Stein, Mr. Simmons."

"Morning, John."

"Our Mr. Willis took his lady friend to dinner last night, Counselor. St. Regis. Long dinner. Didn't get back to her place until almost eleven. And—he left about half an hour ago."

"All right, Johnny. Willis and Grace Carter are sleeping together. And neither is married, so you can't charge them with adultery. What did they have for dinner at the St. Regis, Johnny?"

"*Escargot,* followed by *coq au vin* and *crêpe suzettes.* And coffee and Remy Martin. And you can go to hell, Bernie."

"Laugh when you say that," Bernie said, and John Stein laughed accommodatingly.

"This trooper," Bernie said. "The one who chased the man with all those hundred-dollar bills. Anything more on him, John?"

"Nothing new. Lane caught him just as he was

186

checking in. He's on the eight-to-four, Trooper Turner is. Paul had to get up there around the crack of dawn."

"A policeman's lot is not a happy one. So?"

"He'd pulled off into this Pinetree Lane. All right, to get a few minutes in the shade, as one cop to another. This guy came along in a blue Chevy. Saw the police car, way Turner guessed it. Because he'd slowed down as if he was going to turn into the lane Turner was parked in. But that's only Turner's guessing. Anyway, he didn't turn in. Just took off at 'excessive speed.' Police for 'like a bat out of hell.' So Turner chased the Chevy until it ran into this truck. Says he used his siren and the driver—this guy Pfeiffer—slowed down. Which was why he wasn't killed."

"Or, of course, why he hit the truck," Bernie Simmons said. "If he'd kept on going at this excessive speed, he might have been a mile or two up the road when this truck nosed out. It did nose out in front of him, Johnny?"

"What the trooper said."

"This Pinetree Lane. It does dead-end?"

"Well, pretty much, according to the trooper. What happens is, it stops being paved. There's a barrier, of sorts. Easy enough to get around, trooper says. Dirt road—unimproved, he calls it—for about half a mile. Then it joins a paved highway. Planning to pave the dirt road, Turner says. The township is. Has been planning to for about ten years. Meanwhile, people who know about it use it as a cutoff. Shorter way to Mt. Kisco, if you live near the end of Pinetree."

"I suppose this paved road runs two ways, Johnny?"

"Most roads do, Counselor. Turn left on it and you get to Kisco. Turn right, and you get God knows where. Bangor, Maine, for all I know."

"Or Danbury, Connecticut?"

"Could be, I guess."

"Where this man Pfeiffer said he was going," Bernie said. "At this allegedly excessive speed?"

"What he told the trooper. What the trooper says he told him. Hearsay, obviously."

"Obviously, Counselor," Bernie told his fellow member of the bar, who still planned to go into practice when he retired from the police force.

"So," Stein said. "All I've got at the moment, Bernie."

"At this point in time," Bernie said, "they tried to wreck the republic. And they didn't do the English language any good, did they?"

Stein agreed that they hadn't done the English language any good. He thought the language would survive. He had similar hopes for the country. He said, "You're still not sold on Willis, Assistant District Attorney Simmons?"

"No. You may be right. Probably you are right. But no. Not as assistant district attorney, deputy chief Homicide Bureau."

"We could, anyway, bring him in to answer a few pointed questions. With you sitting in, Bernie."

"And his counsel, John. And leaks to the press about harassment. Not yet, John. Not with what we have to go on. They've got the right to sleep together, Captain."

"Which," Stein said, "could be right profitable for Mr. Willis."

He hung up on that. Bernie sat for a moment and looked at the recradled telephone. Then he buzzed for Mary Leffing. He wanted her to do something for him. Not precisely a routine thing.

"Look up something called Consolidated Communications in the phone book, Mary. Ring them and ask for a Mr. Heslip." He spelled it for her. "Probably in Public Relations, you think. Mr. Raymond Heslip. If they haven't any Mr. Heslip, you're sorry. Some mistake. If they have, and put you through, it isn't a Mr. Raymond Heslip you want. It's a Mr.—oh, Robert Heslip. And again you're oh, so sorry and hang up. O.K.?"

"Yes, Mr. Simmons."

She was halfway through the door when he said, "Oh, Mary," and she turned back.

"If this Consolidated outfit hasn't got any Mr. Heslip, call Bartwell Industries and go through the same routine. O.K.?"

"Yes, Mr. Simmons. Consolidated Communications. Then Bartwell Industries. I'll get right on it."

She closed the door behind her. One of the good things about Mary Leffing was that she didn't want fuller explanations. Not unless there was a need to know. Damn Watergate, from idiotic start to frightening finish. ADA Hiram Snugly—what a name to lug around! —memoed that the city police and the Feds had a drug stakeout going and that the Feds were taking over, so his memo was for information only. ADA Louis Springer had, subject to approval, authorized a homicide charge in the Harrington case. District Attorney Brian Hagerty had authorized with full signature. Bernie added B.S. and put the memo in his Out basket.

Mary Leffing, pro forma, tapped on the door and came in.

"This Raymond Heslip does work for Consolidated Communications, Mr. Simmons. Not in Public Relations. In something called 'Programming.' Only he's on vacation. The operator doesn't know where he can be reached."

"All right, dear. Thanks. You didn't—oh, identify yourself?"

"Far as their switchboard knows, I was a girl friend, just checking up. Or stood up, could be. All right, Ber— Mr. Simmons?"

"Perfectly, Miss Leffing. How's Joe?"

Bernie had never met Joe. He had heard Mary use his name on her telephone. He had heard the note in her voice when she spoke the very ordinary name.

Joe was fine.

Again he stopped her on the way back to her own office.

"Try Bartwell Industries," he said. "Same routine, but a different name this time. Arnold Pfeiffer." He spelled the name. "Probably the Security Division, or whatever they call it."

She said, "Yes, Mr. Simmons." This time she did not close the door between the offices. He lighted a cigarette. He heard her voice, but could not distinguish the words. He heard her replace the telephone. This time she did not come back into his office, but stood in the doorway.

"They haven't got a Mr. Arnold Pfeiffer. They seemed to know that right away. A company that big, you'd think they'd have to check through an employee record, or something. But right away, they'd never heard of a Mr. Pfeiffer."

Bernie said, "Thank you, dear," and Mary went back into her own office. This time, she closed the door after her.

So. Mr. Raymond Heslip, Jr., was on vacation. At Larry's bar, apparently. And Robert Coppell? Perhaps he should have Mary go through the same routine at Consolidated Communications and Bartwell Industries. He didn't think so. Robert Coppell, at a guess, inhabited thin air; was a simulated ghost drifting through Waverly Place at an opportune moment. And on instructions. Whose instructions?

Bartwell Industries had a tall building filled with employees. Hundreds of them, probably. And without looking any of them up, a switchboard operator knew that not one of the hundreds was named Arnold Pfeiffer. I wonder whether, if I called IBC and asked to speak to former Police Captain O'Brien, the operator would assure me instantly that no Captain O'Brien was employed there. Security officers must, of course, be kept secure.

Pinetree Lane didn't actually dead-end beyond the Streeters' house. It was used as a cutoff by people who wanted to get to Mt. Kisco. Or, conceivably, Danbury, Connecticut. By somebody who preferred back roads to parkways or interstates. Well, I do myself, Bernie Simmons thought, and reluctantly took more papers out of the In basket. His telephone rang and he put the papers back in the In basket. He said, "Yes, Mary?" to the telephone.

"Do you want to speak to a Miss Osborne, Mr. Simmons? A Miss Janet Osborne?"

Bernie did indeed.

"Phil, I mean Mr. Whitmore, said to call you if something came up and I couldn't get him," Janet Osborne said. "And I can't get him. He's 'on assignment,' they say. Which means he's doing a think piece and doesn't want to be bothered. Maybe you don't either, Mr.—oh, Mr. Willis. I won't be a—"

"You're at your office, aren't you?" Bernie said.

"Yes, Mr.—"

Bernie Simmons spoke quickly, cutting her off.

"Don't want to tie you up, if Mr. Willis needs you. Suppose you call me back when you're free. And—I suppose there's a telephone booth handy?" He kept his voice low. Voices sometimes carry beyond the ear pressed against the telephone receiver.

"Why, down in the lobby there's—"

"Good. When you're free, call me from a booth. All right?"

"Why, I suppose—"

"As soon as you're free, Miss Osborne," Bernie said, and hung up.

Probably he was being overcautious. The Watergate syndrome persisted. Like a bad cold. Or something much worse than a bad cold. Or was it the White House syndrome? Anyway, there was no real reason to think the phone in Janet Osborne's office was tapped; that a tape might be recording whatever she had to say to an assistant district attorney, County of New York.

Bernie did not go back to the In basket. He lighted a cigarette and waited for the telephone to ring. It did, after only about five minutes, which was probably too soon. "Mr. Hagerty, Mr. Simmons."

Bernie said, "Good morning, sir."

"This Carter case, Mr. Simmons. Reporters getting very—well, insistent. Driving the Commissioner damn near nuts. Starting in on me. Well, Bernard?"

"Maybe, sir. Captain Stein thinks he is on to something. And I've got a call coming through that could be—"

"Making progress," Hagerty said. "Following all leads. You know where that gives the press a pain, don't you, Bernard? And now these TV bas—gentlemen?"

"Yes, Mr. Hagerty. You want me to stick my neck out, sir?"

"Not too far, no. You figure you can?"

"Well, I've got a guess, sir. Nothing solid but—perhaps it's beginning to shape up. A little, anyway."

"We can't get an indictment on guesses," Hagerty said, and then added something surprising to Bernie's ears. "Not even yours, Bernard."

Hagerty hung up with that, leaving Bernard Simmons feeling as if a ritual sword had touched his shoulder and he had been told to arise.

His cigarette had smoldered low in the tray. He lighted a fresh one and waited. It was almost fifteen minutes before the phone rang again. It was also two cigarettes. Which was probably bad for lungs; which was of some help with nerves.

"Miss Osborne is calling, Mr. Simmons."

"A rewrite for 'News Tonight,' Mr. Simmons. On an in-depth bit. I'm sorry I took so long. And probably it isn't—"

"Are you in a booth, Miss Osborne?"

She was in a booth. "And," she said, "one that's off by itself. You're a suspicious man, Mr. Simmons. Cloak-and-dagger, the way Phil was last night."

"And, he tells me, a car almost ran him down. Had to wrap himself in that cloak of his, apparently. You've remembered something, Miss Osborne?"

"It was that picture in the paper this morning," Janet Osborne said. "The one of Dr. Streeter. With the story about his nomination to the FCC. Everybody at IBC is happy about that, Mr. Simmons. From our point of view—from the point of view of all the networks—that Mr. Whiteside would have been, well, a stinker."

"Pleased and surprised, I imagine," Bernie said. "You saw this picture of Paul Streeter and? And what, Miss Osborne?"

"Nothing very important, I'm afraid. Only, Phil said if anything came up. Anything at all."

"Yes?"

"About three years ago," Janet said. "I was still working at Bartwell's. One night I was tied up till late on a report for somebody. Mr. Silcox, I think it was. A Friday evening, as I remember. About seven, I think it was. A little after seven. And I had a date.

I was in a hurry. I—well, I almost ran out of the elevator. And I almost ran into them. Dr. Streeter, I mean. I'm not telling this very well, am I?"

"You're doing fine. You said 'them.' Dr. Streeter and?"

"A man everybody called 'J.J.' One of the brass. I'd seen him with Mr. Lawrence. Mr. Lawrence is the head of Bartwell. The main head. Bartwell has a lot of heads, actually."

"I know. A hydra. Dr. Streeter and this J.J.?"

"A Mr. Jenkins, as I remember it. I don't know his first name."

"Jeremiah," Bernie told her. "He heads up something called Consolidated Communications, if it's the same J.J."

She said "Oh" and held it for a moment. Then she said, "That outfit. They tried to take over IBC a while back. But Clay wouldn't sell out. Persuaded Mr. Graham not to, either. Anyway, I think that was how it was."

"Probably," Bernie said. "You saw this Jenkins and Paul Streeter in the lobby of the Bartwell building about three years ago. Almost ran into them. They were going out, Miss Osborne? As you were?"

"No, they were going in. I said something about being sorry and one of them—J.J., I think—said there was nothing to be sorry about. Something like that. Then they got into the executive elevator. It's express to the twenty-fifth floor. The top floor. Where all the brass has its offices. Where the executive dining room is. Not that I ever saw that, of course."

"They would have been serving dinner in that dining room? Even on Fridays? Was this in the summer, Miss Osborne?"

"It must have been. It was a month or so before

I quit at Bartwell's and got a job at IBC. And that was right after Labor Day."

"Jenkins and Streeter must have got a good look at you. Since, as you say, you almost ran into them."

She supposed so. Then she said, "Wait." He waited, but only for a second.

"Last Saturday," she said. "When Clay took me up there for tennis. When I first met him—or maybe when we were leaving; seems to me it was one of the times we shook hands—Dr. Streeter looked at me as if he thought he had seen me before and couldn't remember where. You know that expression on people's faces, Mr. Simmons? That sort of puzzled expression? It was probably on mine, too."

"But he didn't say, 'Haven't I met you some place before?' Something like that?"

"No. But then neither did I. Probably it didn't bother him the way it did me. After all, I was just a woman Clay had brought along to make the right number for tennis. Not—oh, not worth having second thoughts about. Wondering about."

Bernie Simmons merely said "Mmmm" to that.

"Anyway," Janet said, "now it's off my mind. That Mr. Coppell—although Phil says he's really somebody else—well, he didn't seem quite right. Not after I'd thought it over, I mean. But it's all straight, now. And probably, it wasn't worth bothering you with. Only, Phil did say 'anything.' "

"I'm very glad you bothered me," Bernie said. "Mr. Willis came into your office while you were first talking to me, I gather?"

"Yes. About a rewrite."

"Do you think he knew who you were talking to?"

"I don't know. Maybe I mentioned your name. But perhaps if I did it was before he came in. Why?"

"Probably doesn't matter, one way or the other, Miss Osborne. Only—well, I'd just as soon you didn't mention your having remembered where you met Paul Streeter. Or having told me about it."

"All right. Not to anybody at all?"

"Oh," he said, "Phil Whitmore, of course. I meant, not anybody at your office."

Again she said, "All right." But then she said, "It all seems so trivial, somehow. But all right, Mr. Simmons."

"Probably is," Bernie said. "But anyway, it's off your mind now. Go back up and finish that rewrite, Miss Osborne."

"Oh, I finished that before I came down to the lobby. It was quite short and Mr. Willis wanted it right away. The Australians wanted to see it before it went on the air. It's a piece about aborigines."

What this morning needs is aborigines, Bernie thought, as he put the telephone in its cradle. Maybe they had it better. Anyway, they sure as hell had it simpler. He reached toward the In basket. The *Chronicle* was still spread across his desk, folded open at page 48. He glanced down at it.

a definitive work.

Although a Californian by birth, Dr. Streeter is a member of a family long established in upper New York State. His father, the late Dr. Harrington Streeter, a neurosurgeon, moved to San Francisco in the early 1920's. Paul Streeter was born there in 1925. His father had an extensive practice in his adopted state and in 1929 was head of the county medical society. He suffered substantial financial losses in the Depression and on his death in 1932, his young wife—the former Evelyn Farmer of Albany, New York—and their young son were left in straitened circumstances.

Paul Streeter worked at a variety of jobs during his high-school and college years. "Almost everything you can think of," he said in a recent interview. "Everything a kid could do. Threw papers, collected insurance payments, mowed grass for people. You name it and I did it. I even got a job fixing radios when I was about seventeen. That didn't last long. The radios didn't stay fixed long, I'm afraid. In college I did some tutoring. Sound sort of like a latter-day Horatio Alger number, don't I?"

Whether or not Paul Streeter was a "latter-day Horatio Alger number," he was a brilliant student at Berkeley, both as an undergraduate and as a graduate. He was magna cum laude and Phi Beta Kappa. His doctor's thesis, published by the Yale University Press, had a readership by no means limited to the academic community.

His father's sister Emily—known affectionately for many years in Albany as The Miss Streeter—continued to live in the ancestral Streeter house until her death some two years ago at the age of ninety-three. She continued active until a few months before her death and her "at homes," as they were called by her generation, were still an established feature of Albany's Friday afternoons until a year or so before her death. "I suppose you'd have to call Aunt Emily a grande dame," Dr. Streeter said in his interview, on the occasion of his appointment to the Edward R. Murrow Chair at Dyckman. "She was also the owner of what must have been one of the few extant electric automobiles. Drove it herself, pretty much all over town. Had a habit of parking it in front of fire hydrants. I doubt if she ever got a summons. Everybody knew her and her electric, including the police. Particularly the police, I suppose. Aunt Emily was what used to be called an 'original.'"

The Streeter house is in what was for many years a fashionable section of Albany. The neighborhood had deteriorated while Miss Streeter still lived there. "I used to try to get her to move," Dr. Streeter says. "I wasted my breath." What was once sometimes called the "Streeter Mansion" is now a rooming house.

Bernie folded the *Chronicle* and reached it toward his wastebasket. He did not drop it in. He put it back, neatly folded, on his desk. He looked at his still-bulging In basket. But he did not really see it. He reached toward the buzzer which would summon Mary Leffing. He did not press it.

Instead, he got up from his desk and went to the door between his office and hers. She looked up when he opened the door and said, "Yes, Mr. Simmons?"

"I'd like you to put in a call for me," Bernie said. "Out-of-town call. To Leslie Franklin in the D.A.'s office in Albany. And if he's in court, leave word asking him to call me back."

She said, "Yes, Mr. Simmons."

13

BERNIE HAD TO WAIT only about ten minutes for his desk phone to ring. "I have Mr. Franklin, Mr. Simmons. Go ahead, Mr. Franklin."

Leslie Franklin went ahead. He said, "Hi, Bernie. How's tricks?"

They had met at Lake Placid the summer before, when district attorneys and their assistants had gathered to listen to, among other things, a justice of the United States Supreme Court discuss crime prevention. An appointee of the current Administration, he had been inclined to blame crime on "permissiveness."

Bernie did not answer the "How's tricks" query. He thought it best forgotten. He hoped he hadn't dragged an assistant district attorney, Albany County, out of court.

"Recessed for the summer," Leslie Franklin said. "We twiddle thumbs. And think about indictments.

Something on your mind, Counselor?"

"A Miss Streeter," Bernie said. "Quite a character up your way, from what I read."

"If you mean Miss Emily, all of that. A part of the city's history. That electric of hers. See it coming and you drove up onto sidewalks. What about her, Bernard? She's been dead a couple of years. Oh, about her nephew?"

"More or less," Bernie said. "I gather she was a rich woman?"

"So did everybody. Hell of a big surprise when the assessment came out. Surprising it didn't make more of a splash in the press. *Noblesse oblige,* maybe, which you don't expect from the press. Say—maybe they're just tumbling to it. Friend of mine over at the surrogate's office—man named Blinkenstop; nice guy—says a reporter was asking around about her a couple of weeks ago. Correspondent for a TV network, Blinky says this guy was. Where was I, Counselor?"

"Miss Emily Streeter, Les. *The* Miss Streeter. Tumbling to what, Leslie?"

"That everybody assumed she had the stuff in wads, when actually she died damn near broke. Came out when the assessment was filed. For tax purposes. Matter of public record, you know."

Bernie did know. Did Leslie Franklin happen to have any figures?

"Not my line of country. Blinky looked it up for this TV man. Gave me the figures. Rough figures, anyway. According to Blinky, she left something like eight thousand dollars. In a checking account. And the house, of course. Big, ramshackle old place. And, now, pretty much in the middle of a slum. Court-appointed executor sold it for around ten thousand, according to Blinky. Glad to get that much, probably."

"Not much of an estate," Bernie said. "Any idea who got it, Les?"

"The woman who lived with her," Franklin said. "Old woman Miss Streeter called her housekeeper. Almost as old as Emily herself. Been there for years, my father says. He used to go to those 'at homes' of hers. Years ago, that would have been. Used to have quite a staff, Dad says. Dwindled down to this old biddy. Probably there was a lot of money there once but—well, there you are."

"There Miss Streeter was," Bernie said. "She outlived it. This TV man who got hold of your friend. Network man, you say?"

"What he told Blinky, apparently. Local affiliate, probably."

"Affiliate of?"

Franklin wasn't sure he remembered. He thought maybe IBC.

For almost a minute, Bernie regarded the telephone. His gaze was reproachful. But it was not the telephone his mind reproached; his mind rejected what increasingly seemed to be the facts. His hope that Johnny Stein would turn out to be right was diminishing.

He got the Manhattan telephone directory out of a bottom desk drawer. What had this man Pfeiffer—the man who carried hundred-dollar bills around; the man with the credentials of a licensed private investigator—said the name of his firm was? Conover and something improbable. He turned back through his notes, on memo slips clipped together. "Conover & Comfortobelli." Shortened to "ConCom." (Understandably; no firm would want to be confused with a digestive pill.) "ConCom Investigations." With an address in the West Forties.

He pressed the appropriate button in the base of the telephone. He got the dial tone. He dialed. The ringing signal sounded four times and a precise female voice came through. "This is the operator. What number did you dial, please?" He told her what number he had dialed and got, "One moment, please." He waited the moment. "The number you have dialed is not a working number, sir."

He hung up and shook his head at the telephone. He dialed again. He got "Independent Broadcasting Company; may I help you?" He asked for Miss Janet Osborne. After three rings, "Miss Osborne. Good morning."

"Simmons. Mind dropping down to that phone booth again? Oh, and good morning to you, too."

"Well, I'm supposed to be working, Mr. Simmons."

"Time for elevenses," Bernie said. "And I won't keep you long."

She said, "Well, all right."

He hung up and waited. He waited a little less than ten minutes. Mary said, "Miss Janet Osborne is calling, Mr. Simmons."

Janet said, "All right. I'm in a booth. And it's stifling. And why do you think my phone's tapped?"

"Just not taking chances, Miss Osborne. Shouldn't take more than a couple of minutes. The Streeter place, where we met Saturday. You hadn't ever been there before, had you?"

"No."

"Do you know whether Carter had?"

He waited a few seconds for her answer.

"I don't think so," she said. "Wait—no, I'm sure he hadn't. He had to use a map to get there. They haven't lived there long. They had a housewarming party two or three weeks ago and Clay was invited but couldn't go because it was on Friday evening and he had to be on the air."

"Did he seem to be surprised by—oh, the size of the place? The general—oh, affluent setup?"

"I don't know about Clay. I was. Clay'd told me Dr. Streeter was a college professor. The place looked like a lot of money. To me, anyway. Wasn't there something about a rich aunt dying and leaving him money?"

"Yes. So far's you know, Carter hadn't seen the place before? Wouldn't have known what to expect?"

"Unless friends of his who'd been to this housewarming party had told him about it."

"And this party was two or three weeks ago?"

"That's what Clay said, Mr. Simmons. We were there—oh, sort of on a rain check, I guess. Like you and Miss Curran?"

"No. We weren't invited to the housewarming. Thank you, my dear. You can go back to air conditioning."

Bernie put the receiver back on its prongs. He sat and looked at it. He lighted a cigarette. He had better pass it on to Johnny Stein. He lifted the receiver and got the dial tone instead of Mary Leffing. He buzzed for Mary Leffing. She said, "If you'll press the other button, Mr. Simmons." He pressed the button. "Captain Stein," Mary said, confirming. "And if he's out, Detective Lane. Right away, Mr. Simmons."

He looked at his In basket. In baskets are presumably necessary; they can also be a damn bore. He reached toward it and the telephone tinkled.

Captain John Stein was not in his office at Homicide, Manhattan North. Detective Paul Lane was not at his desk in the squad room. Did he want to talk to Lieutenant Sullivan? He did not want to talk to Lieutenant Sullivan.

"See if you can get me Mr. Bernstein, dear."

This time there was no waiting. "Securities Bureau, Bernstein."

"Bernie Simmons, Manny. What do you know about a Consolidated Communications Corporation?"

"Clean by us, Bernie. Like a hound's tooth."

"It is—is what, Manny?"

"Owns a lot of radio stations. Middle West and West Coast, mostly. Birchite, I understand. But it's a free country, they tell me. Listed on the American Exchange. Want to know what it closed at yesterday?"

"Not especially. Anyway, I've got a paper in front of me. Not involved in any monkey business, Manny?"

"Not that's reached us. Perfectly legal, right-wing setup. Oh, challenge to one of their stations a year or so ago, as I recall it. Violation of the fairness doctrine. Anti-Semitism, I think it was. Kept its license, as I remember. Oh, and it's a subsidiary of Bartwell Industries. As what isn't?"

"ITT, for one. Thanks, Manny."

Bernie returned to the In basket. It continued to be as dull as it had been. Twice, Mary Leffing came in to add to it. It took an hour and a half, and too many cigarettes, to get to the bottom. It was eleven-thirty when the telephone tinkled. Captain Stein was on the line. He said, "Morning, Counselor." Bernie said, "Hi, John."

"Nothing much," Stein said. "Been checking a few things out. Evidence for your consideration, and not much of it. This detective agency. Two-man operation, essentially. Roger Conover and Anthony Comfortobelli. Been in business fifteen years or so. Not a big operation. Mostly handling jewel-theft recoveries for insurance companies. In other words, paying off jewel thieves. Some internal security jobs for corporations.

Not the kind of outfit maybe you read about. Hasn't ever solved any murders we know of. Neither Conover or Comfortobelli ever got beaten up, far's we know. Comfortobelli didn't die of alcoholism."

"He did die?"

"Three years ago, about. Heart attack."

"Conover carried on? By himself?"

"For a while. Then he sold it. Don't know who to. There's one thing. Their telephone's inoperative. Not a 'working' number, the operator says."

"Yes, John. What she said to me, too."

"All right, Counselor. Precinct man's gone around to knock on their door. See if they've folded up. Check them out with the people who own the building. Etcetera and etcetera."

"But they're clean, far's you've found out?"

"Yes. And so's this man Pfeiffer, as far as the records go. The man who was carrying around all that money up in Westchester. License in order. No complaints pending. And, by the way, on this speeding summons. He sent it in, along with a check to cover the fine—rather more than cover it, as a matter of fact."

"So he won't be showing up for a hearing, John?"

"The idea, obviously. He's back in town, apparently. Anyway, the envelope was postmarked New York, New York."

"Any note with the check? On a letterhead?"

"No. Just a check. Drawn on Chemical. Personal check, with his name and number on it."

"No address?"

"Chemical doesn't print depositors' addresses on their checks. And yes, Bernie. Before you tell us our business, we're getting Mr. Pfeiffer's address from Chemical. Doing our little routine chores, Counselor."

"I'm sure of it, Captain."

"O.K. More to the point, Lane's been around for a little chat with Mrs. Grace Carter, the wealthy widow. Does she happen to remember where she was Saturday afternoon and Saturday night? Until around—oh, one o'clock Sunday morning. The garage picked Carter's car up at twelve-forty Sunday morning, according to their records."

"Did she remember, John?"

"Very clearly. Willis picked her up in a car about four-thirty Saturday afternoon. They drove up to the country to get out of the heat. Had dinner at a perfectly charming restaurant. She doesn't remember exactly where. But such a delightful place. Mr. Willis is so good about finding charming restaurants. After dinner, they drove around some more. It was cool, finally. They could even turn off the car's air conditioning. And, no, they didn't happen to run into anybody they knew. And it must have been almost midnight when they got back to her apartment. They had a nightcap and Willis went home. He has an apartment in the East Seventies, she thinks. No, she doesn't really know exactly where. Lane's gone to IBC to ask Willis if he remembers it the same way. Entirely a matter of routine, of course."

"Of course, John. And he will, of course."

John Stein didn't doubt it.

"And it may be precisely what they did do, John."

Stein said, "Mmmm." Then he said, "Mrs. Carter— or the executors of Carter estate, I suppose—has fired Cyril Johnson. Closing up the house. That 'dreadful white elephant,' she calls it. And Johnson wants to go back home to Jamaica. Says, 'I find it safer there.' All right with your office, Bernie? We've got his statement."

"He'll have to come back for the trial," Bernie said. "Until then, it's O.K. by us."

"If we get to a trial, Counselor. This story of Mrs. Carter's. Well, Bernie. And all that lovely money she gets. And that maybe Willis will marry. Know what they call Willis at the network, Counselor?"

Bernie didn't.

"God Wills, they call him. Well—"

"Closing up the house, you say, John?"

"And draining the swimming pool."

"What about the cat? Or is Johnson adopting him?"

"No. Oh, he's fond of the cat. But it was always Mr. Carter's cat. And Mrs. Carter's allergic to cats, or something. So, ASPCA, I suppose. Johnson wants to take off day after tomorrow. Catch a morning plane."

Bernie said, "All right, John."

"Well," Stein said, "all we've got for—"

Bernie interrupted him. Bernie said, "Wait a minute."

I haven't got much, Bernie thought. I haven't, in fact, got more than half enough, if I've got that. Actually, we've got more—potentially more—on Willis and Grace Carter. I'll be leading with my chin. And with John's chin. Based pretty much on what I'm guessing—guessing from, of all things, on what I've seen on a tennis court. If I'm wrong, the chief will scalp me. Come to that, he'll probably fire me.

"We'll need a car, John," Bernie said. "A nice, unobtrusive car. With air conditioning, preferably. I'll rent one, if the NYPD would rather. County expense, rather than city expense."

John Stein said, "What the hell, Bernie?" which was not unexpected.

"A little drive in the country," Bernie said. "It's supposed to be cooler in the country."

"Not in the middle of the day," John Stein told

him. "And we don't even know the name of this restaurant they had dinner at. Unless Lane's come up with it. And, for God's sake, we've got men out on half a dozen cases. You got the idea Carter's is the only killing up in the air?"

"No, John. A police car, or do I rent one?"

He couldn't give orders to Detective Captain John Stein, New York Police Department. All he could do was assess evidence the police brought in; decide what charge, if any, it warranted. As Stein was, of course, waiting to tell him.

"You're nuts," Stein said. "Like always, you're nuts. Lane too?"

"It might be a good idea, John."

"I'll order a car," Stein said. "I can't guarantee air conditioning. I suppose you want us to come down and pick you up, Counselor?"

Bernie Simmons said he could just as well take a taxi. He said they could just as well have lunch on the way up. "Courtesy District Attorney, New York County," Bernie said, and hoped it would be . . .

The car was black and unmarked. It was also air-conditioned. "Inspector's car," Stein said, as Lane drove them north on the West Side Highway, on the Henry Hudson, on the Parkway. "The old boy's on vacation. Up on the Cape somewhere. All right, Counselor. Give."

Bernie gave. Stein, as he listened, at first said, "Mmmm?" After a time he merely said, "Mmmm." When Bernie said, "That's it, John," Stein looked at the back of Paul Lane's neck for almost a minute before he said, "When you come down to it, it isn't much, is it? Not as much, actually, as we've got on Willis and his girl friend. We're sticking our necks out, don't you think?"

"Possibly," Bernie said. "Even probably. What we're paid for, isn't it?"

"One way of looking at it," Stein said. "I hope we don't pay with the same necks."

"We've stuck them out before," Bernie said. "Our heads are still on them."

Stein said, "Yeah." There was no enthusiasm in his voice.

They pulled off the Parkway for lunch. At Bernie's suggestion, they did not hurry over it. While they ate, Bernie filled in Detective Paul Lane. When he is driving, Paul Lane keeps his attention on the road. Especially when he is driving an inspector's car.

Lane told them that Willis confirmed Grace Carter's account of their Saturday afternoon and night. He gave them the address Chemical, New York, had for Arnold Pfeiffer. Stein found a telephone and used it.

It was a little after two in the afternoon when, at Bernard Simmons's suggestion, Lane pulled the car onto the shoulder a little short of the Streeters' driveway. Bernie and John Stein waited at the foot of the drive while Lane walked toward the house on the grass; walked to it and around it on the side opposite the tennis court. There was nobody in sight. When Lane had gone around the corner of the house, Bernie and John Stein walked up the drive. They did not hurry. They had gone only a few yards when they heard the sharp ping of tennis balls against rackets. The players, Bernie thought, were hitting cleanly. From the sounds, there were only two players.

They walked quietly, on the grass beside the graveled drive. When they were halfway between road and house, Bernie touched Stein's arm, guiding. They went off to the right, walking on closely mowed lawn. The canvas of the backstop kept them from the view of the players on the court. They went some distance beyond the house and the adjacent tennis court before they circled back to a point from which they could watch Agnes and Paul Streeter playing singles—playing, Bernie thought, rather diligently.

They watched the players for several minutes. Streeter was playing the sun court. He was using only his second service. His drives were deep, but not hard. And he was winning, although not by much. "Five-three," Streeter told his wife and bounced three balls to her. She served, obviously as hard as she could serve.

"See what I mean?" Bernie said, his voice low.

"He's better than she is," Stein said.

"Yes. He's not going all out, of course. Friendly family game, primarily for exercise. Keep on looking, John."

They kept on watching the game; watching Agnes, in a short white dress and Paul Streeter in white shorts and shirt. "Good-looking couple," John Stein said.

"Yes. But watch the game, John. I told you what to watch for."

They watched while Agnes finished her service game. It went to deuce twice, but she won it.

"Only thing I can see," Stein said, "she seems to hit it where he is. Where he can hit back, I mean."

"Yes," Bernie said. "But turn it around, John. He gets where she's going to hit it. Thinks ahead of her, most of the time, anyway. There. See that."

Streeter had served, rather gently, to his wife's forehand. She returned, deep but not hard, to his backhand. He ran around to take it on his forehand, and drove straight down the line. Then he went in toward the net. He did not run across toward the center of the court, but more or less up along the sideline.

This left a large area of the court enticingly open for Agnes's return.

She was not enticed. She tried a down the line shot, which, if Streeter had moved to his right to cover against a cross-court, would have caught him going the wrong way.

He had not. He was waiting for her drive. He won the point with a stop volley.

"Damn you," Agnes said, gaiety in her voice, "you were supposed to be going the other way."

"She's said it for you," Bernie said. "He was a thought ahead of her. He guessed what she was going to try."

"Probably," Stein said, "they've played each other a good deal. Know—well, each other's tricks."

"Oh," Bernie said, "that enters in, yes. But I've played him, John. Not often, but enough to get an idea of his game. He anticipates her shots, yes. He also anticipated mine. At first, anyway. It's a good part of the game, John—given reasonable equality of strokes, ability to anticipate what your opponent is going to try can make the difference. Lots of things can make the difference, including bad bounces. Those tend to even out. An ability to think ahead of the other guy doesn't. Paul Streeter thinks a long way ahead. The chance always is, with him, that wherever you put the ball, he'll be there waiting. Having thought a jump ahead of you."

"You make him sound pretty good, Bernie."

"Oh, not all that good, John. There's such a thing as thinking too far ahead. Such a thing as too much anticipation. Seems a shame to break it up, John, but I guess we'd better."

They walked across the smoothly mowed lawn toward the tennis court and the two walking off it toward chairs waiting in the shade.

Paul Streeter was the first to see them. He stopped abruptly, just short of the deck chair he had obviously been heading for. He did not sit in the chair, but stood beside it and looked at them. For a few seconds, Bernie thought, there was rigidity in Paul Streeter's face. But then his lips moved in what, clearly, was to be taken as a welcoming smile.

He turned to his wife. He said, "Look who's here, darling."

But, to Bernie Simmons's ears, the tone of his voice did not match the cheerfulness of his words.

Agnes Streeter looked at them. There was, Bernie thought, surprise in her face; more surprise than had showed on her husband's face. "Why, how nice," Agnes Streeter said. "What a pleasant surprise, Bernie."

Bernie said they were sorry to break in; sorry to interrupt their game.

"Oh, we'd finished," Agnes said. "Every afternoon we—"

Paul Streeter's voice cut sharply across his wife's, anticipating what she had been going to say; at the same time dismissing it. He said, "A social call, Simmons?"

He moves too fast, Bernie thought. He jumps at it.

"No, Doctor," Bernie said, glad Streeter had been the first to break from friendly familiarity. "Not a social call. This is Captain Stein. Mrs. Streeter. Dr. Streeter."

Agnes said, "Captain Stein," in the voice of a hostess being introduced to a guest. "So—" But she stopped with that, and looked at her husband. He was looking at the two men standing in front of him. There was, Bernie thought, watchfulness in Paul Streeter's eyes. But perhaps, of course, he merely hoped there was.

"Police captain, Doctor," Bernie said. "We think

there may be one or two things you can help us with. In connection with Clayton Carter's death. His quite unanticipated death."

Streeter shook his head. He said, his voice low and steady, that he didn't get it.

"If it's about that TV set of his," Streeter said, "I told you all I know about that. It was all right when I carried it up to his car. All charged up and ready to go."

"I remember what you told me," Bernie said. "That you unplugged the set and accidentally turned it on, proving it hadn't been tampered with on your terrace. And that you carried it up to Carter's car for him. You had a flashlight in your other hand, as I remember it."

"The lights were off on the terrace then. What's the flashlight got to do with it?"

"Nothing, probably," Bernie said. "Easier to see what you're doing with a light, of course. Did he get the money to you, Doctor? And why don't we all sit down?"

Streeter did not sit down. He did not appear to have heard the suggestion. He said, "What the hell are you talking about, Simmons?" His voice had gone higher. He might have been talking to a man some yards from him, instead of only a few feet. "What money? And who's 'he'?"

"A man named Pfeiffer, Doctor. And a good many hundred-dollar bills. I don't know how many. We'll have to ask Mr. Pfeiffer that. Unless you want to tell us how much they've been paying you. As what, Doctor? A consultant? Is that what they called it?"

Streeter didn't know what the hell Simmons was talking about. His voice was strident now.

"Money," Bernie said. "Money in nice crisp hundreds. The kind of money you used to buy this place of yours. Complete with tennis court and swimming pool. All the comforts of wealth. Cost several times what a professor earns in a year, at a guess."

"All of which is none of your damn business, Simmons. Not that there's any secret about it. A rich aunt of mine—"

He stopped speaking because Bernard Simmons was shaking his head slowly and with a kind of finality.

"No," Bernie said. "Not Aunt Emily Streeter of Albany. She left only a few thousand, Doctor. And she didn't leave it to you. Left it to a servant-companion who'd been with her for years. Carter found out about that, didn't he? Had an IBC stringer in Albany check it out? Somebody tip you off to that, Doctor? And give you the idea Carter might louse up the whole deal? The whole sweet deal, which was going to lift IBC's local license and put it down in the lap of Consolidated Communications? When you got on the FCC and swung the majority that way?"

"That damn girl!" Streeter said. "That God-damn spying bitch. That—"

"If you're talking about Miss Janet Osborne," Bernie said, "she's a very nice person, Doctor. And Carter didn't bring her up here to put the finger on you. Just brought her up to fill out a mixed doubles team, was all. You recognized her right away, didn't you? Supposed she'd recognize you from that time a few years back when she saw you going into the Bartwell building with Jenkins. Figured you'd better move before Carter did? That was it, wasn't it? Did you use one of those steak knives of yours to scrape insulation off the wire in the TV set? The one with the little nick in the edge which left a mark on the wire? So that the lab boys think they probably can identify the knife? The knife, by the way, that came with my steak—my damn good steak—Saturday night."

Streeter seemed about to speak, but he did not speak. Instead, he sat down in the deck chair. But Agnes Streeter spoke.

"You couldn't have had that knife," Agnes said. "We know about it, of course. We've been meaning to have it ground down. We're always very careful not to give it to guests. I'm sure either Paul or I had it Saturday evening. We're always very careful about things—"

She let it hang there. She sat on one of the director's chairs. She looked at her husband. Bernie thought she was looking at him as if she had never seen him before. But that, he thought, is probably only my imagination at work.

He decided against telling Paul Streeter that Janet Osborne hadn't recognized him last Saturday; had merely had a vague, troubling notion that she had seen him somewhere before— and that, if events had not made an issue of it, she probably would never have remembered seeing him and Jeremiah Jenkins getting into an express elevator in the Bartwell building. Certainly she couldn't have guessed Paul Streeter was being offered a job as consultant with Consolidated Communications–Bartwell Industries.

He thought Streeter had had enough for the moment without being told that he had anticipated too far ahead—anticipated to a murder not really that hurriedly necessary.

Stein beckoned to Detective Lane, now in sight standing by the swimming pool, so that Lane could go with Streeter while the man who wasn't, after all, going to be confirmed as a member of the Federal Communications Commission changed from tennis clothes to something more suitable for a trip into the city.

14

IT WAS TEN MINUTES after seven when Bernie Simmons rang the doorbell of Apartment 5J in East Fifty-second Street and heard the ruthless jangle inside. He had said seven; he hadn't done too badly, considering everything—considering the still unabated heat; considering most of the night before and the court hearing at ten in the morning.

Nora looked cool in a sleeveless green and white dress. She looked—a word came into Bernie's mind which had been buried there since boyhood—Nora Curran looked scrumptious. He didn't tell her that, although he looked the word toward her. What Bernie said was, "Whew!"

"You look wilted down," Nora said, with that honesty sometimes possible between lovers. "Sit down there, and I'll make us drinks." "There" was in front of a window air conditioner, and Bernie did as he was told.

Nora brought drinks and they clicked glasses and she said, "It doesn't seem possible. I thought he was a nice man."

"A good many unpleasant things are possible," Bernie told her. "Even complicated things. Even conspiracies. You make a fine martini, darling."

"I've had a good teacher," she said. "I've been reading the papers. The *Chronicle* this morning and the *Post* this afternoon. They leave things up in the air. Dr. Paul Streeter, Dyckman University professor, was questioned at some length last night by homicide detectives, with a representative of the District Attorney's office present. Dr. Streeter was charged with homicide this morning in criminal court. He pleaded not guilty and was bound over for action by the grand jury. His attorney's application for release in bond was denied by Judge Somebody-or-other."

"Langster," Bernie told her. "Judge Langster. The grand jury in—oh, about a week, probably. When we get things pulled together."

She nodded her head and waited.

"Streeter wanted a nice place in the country," Bernie said. "He thought he'd be able to buy one when his rich aunt died. He'd been thinking that for years, looking forward to it for years. Turned out his aunt wasn't rich at all. He doesn't admit any of this, of course. He doesn't admit anything. Not even that this Consolidated Communications outfit offered him a job as a consultant at sixty thousand a year. With a further incentive—if he played along with the team, he'd get the next vacancy on the FCC."

"They could promise that?"

"Well, he got it. Late this afternoon. The appointment turned out to be inoperative. That's the word the press secretary used—'inoperative.' Also 'Complete confidence that Dr. Streeter would have turned out to be an admirable public servant, and was innocent until proved guilty, in spite of insinuations in the news media, which is obviously prejudging and denying this distinguished scholar a fair trial.' "

"Because it reported what happened, Bernie? Shall I make us another drink?"

"We're going uptown for dinner," Bernie said. "I've rented a car. Oh, all right. A small one."

She made them each a small one, and sat down again on the sofa beside Bernie. And also, she smells scrumptious, Bernie thought. They clicked glasses.

"Until proved guilty," Nora said. "Will he be?"

"Up to the jury," Bernie said. "He's got a good lawyer. Motive. Opportunity. Not exclusive opportunity. That damn TV set was lying around loose quite a while, and Fred Branson—that's Streeter's lawyer—will rub that in plenty. As I would in his case. And juries don't like technical evidence much. Like expert testimony by the lab people—that the nick in Streeter's steak knife matches scratches on a wire. Bores jurors, that sort of thing does. But we've got a private detective named Pfeiffer who'll testify that for a year and a half he's been delivering cash to Streeter and that, during that time, the total came to ninety thousand and that, yes, he counted it, because he wasn't going to be the fall guy for anybody. And Jeremiah Jenkins will testify that, yes, Consolidated Communications employed Professor Streeter as a consultant and that they did so because he was highly qualified and that it was a perfectly legitimate arrangement and that he was paid in cash because he wanted it that way. And that the fact, which is a matter of record, that his company was trying to get the license now held by the IBC local station is entirely irrelevant. And that he, for one, couldn't have been more surprised when Streeter's appointment to the FCC was announced by the White House. I'm talking myself dry. And probably talking you numb."

He finished his drink. When she raised her eyebrows, he shook his head.

"And Mr. Carter found out about this—arrangement, and was going to—well, break the story?"

"Blow the whistle," Bernie said. "Anyway, Streeter thought he had found out. Oh, probably Streeter was right. Carter had arranged to have dinner with the head of IBC Sunday evening, probably to fill him in. And Carter's phone was tapped. Jenkins's security boys may have found out something and passed it on. But that's guessing. Carter had had a network stringer in Albany check out on Emily Streeter's estate. That we can prove. And Janet Osborne will testify she saw Streeter and this man Jenkins get into the executive elevator together in the Bartwell building, which suggests but doesn't prove. Although the probability that she could—well, it scared Streeter into murder. It made him believe Carter was setting him up. And Carter wasn't, she says. Nothing about Streeter had come up until Saturday afternoon, when they were driving up to play tennis. And then only who he was—the things one likes to find out in advance about a host. So—shall we be on our way?"

It was unlike him, Nora thought. They took their time over drinks always. Tonight he was keyed up; ridden, she thought, by some urgency. She said, "Of course," and stood up. The rented car cooled quickly with the air conditioning turned on. Bernie drove, with more conscious care than was usual with him, up Sixth Avenue. He turned into the Hippodrome garage.

When he took the ticket, Bernie said, "We'll want it on Forty-third in—oh, hour and a half or so." The attendant said, "Yessir," and they crossed Forty-fourth to the Algonquin.

Usually, when they went there they had drinks in the lobby, which now, as always, was almost filled with relaxed people and the tinkle of summoning bells. Nora hesitated for a moment, but Bernie touched her arm and they went on to the entrance of the Oak Room. Robert, the maître d', said, "Good evening, Mr. Simmons. All ready for you," and they followed him to the table for two at the end of the bar—one of the tables held for favorite customers. (And customers Robert wanted to be in view.)

He's got something on his mind tonight, Nora thought. He's got something planned. Robert himself, without being told, brought them martinis in frosted glasses. Again they clicked glasses together.

"All right, darling," Nora said. "What are you up to?"

"Up to?" Bernie said. But then he smiled widely at her and nodded his head. "All right," he said. "We've got sort of a date after dinner. Something I want to show you. And I said around nine or a little after." They ordered; they did not have second drinks. It was only a quarter of nine when they finished coffee and Bernie signed the checks. It was slow going through Forty-third to the West Side Highway. It was faster after that. It was twenty after nine when Bernie edged the car to the curb in front of a tall, thin house on Riverside Drive.

"*Bernie!*" Nora said. "Isn't this—?"

"Yes," he said. "Clayton Carter's house. His wife's house, now."

She said, "Why on earth?" and hesitated for a

second, but his hand on her arm urged her on across the sidewalk, and to a door opening for them.

Cyril Johnson was not in the semiuniform of a man-servant. He wore a pale green sports jacket and dark red slacks which flared at the bottoms. He said, "Good evening, sir. Miss—"

"Miss Curran," Bernie told him. "This is Mr. Johnson, Nora. He's—he was—Mr. Carter's—oh, major domo."

"Valet, Mr. Simmons. Houseman. I'm afraid he knows something's up. I had to close the doors to keep him out from under beds. If you'll both come in here, sir. And we'll have to watch the door."

They went into the long, cool living room. Mao was asleep on one of the sofas beside the fireplace. He slept curled up. But when they went into the room he flowed out of the curl and looked hard at them through very large blue eyes. Then, in what appeared to be one incredibly fluid motion, he went under the sofa. He left his long dark-brown tail outside for a moment. Then he drew it, too, into safety.

"I can get a broom, sir," Johnson said. "But if you and Miss Curran would care to wait, he'll maybe come out. Sometimes he gets to wondering what's going on. Sometimes he comes to find out. I could get you something to drink while we wait? Mr. Carter had some excellent cognac. Or something else, perhaps? A crème de menthe for you, Miss Curran?"

Bernie did not need to look at Nora's face. He knew the expression of mild horror which would be spreading over it.

"Cognac will be fine," Bernie said. "And for yourself, of course."

Johnson said, "Thank you, sir," and went to the end of the room. He came back with a bottle and three small balloon glasses on a silver tray. He poured for them, and was thanked, and poured into the third glass. He went around the coffee table and sat on the other side. He sat on the edge of it and waited to lift his glass until Nora and Bernie had sipped from theirs.

The Siamese cat named Mao stayed under the sofa except for his tail, which reappeared.

"They do sometimes forget about their tails," Nora said. "Diogenes often did. Diogenes was a cat I used to have, Mr. Johnson. A long time ago, when I was a little girl. He used to hide under things and leave his tail sticking out. He was a nice cat."

She spoke in a low, soft voice, an almost crooning voice.

"What is this cat's name, Mr. Johnson?"

Johnson told her the name of the hiding cat.

"Mao," Nora said. "Mao. You're a nice cat, Mao. A lovely cat. A handsome Siamese cat."

The tip of the protruding brown tail twitched.

"Nice Mao," Nora said. (Her voice isn't that tender when she speaks to me, Bernie thought. Of course, I don't hide under sofas.) "Pretty Mao."

The brown tail swirled to one side and vanished. But then a brown-masked face appeared where the tail had been. Then all of Mao appeared, much more slowly than earlier he had vanished. He sat, within one move of the sofa, and looked at Nora.

"Pretty Mao," Nora said. "You're a pretty cat."

Mao decided it was time to wash his face. He washed his face. His tail needed washing. He washed his tail. Reflectively, he scratched behind his right ear. He stretched forelegs out in front of him, gripped the rug and stretched, a little elaborately. Nora told him he was a good cat, and he sat erect and twitched the tip of his tail. Then, a gentleman of leisure, groomed for the evening, he glided under the coffee table and sat again, looking up at Nora Curran—looking intently from unblinking slitted eyes.

"Pretty Mao. Pretty cat," Nora said, in the softest of voices. She reached her right hand down toward the cat, being careful that the hand was in front of him. He looked at the waiting hand. Then he smelled it. Then, gently and briefly, he licked the hand.

"I'd forgotten what abrasive tongues they have," Nora murmured, to nobody in particular. "Like little graters, almost."

Satisfied about the hand, Mao smelled Nora's shoes. This took a little longer. Then he sat again, and looked up at Nora.

"If you want to, Mao," Nora said, and the long cat floated up to her lap. He turned around twice and stretched, with his head between her knees. He began to purr. The whole cat vibrated with the purring.

"Well," Cyril Johnson said. "That is very unlike him, Miss Curran. Usually—" He left that unfinished.

"Captain Stein says you're going back to Jamaica, Mr. Johnson," Bernie said.

"Yes, Mr. Simmons. Tomorrow. Mr. Carter was generous to me in his will, his solicitors say. Most generous. He was a very generous man, sir."

There was, Bernie thought, carefully controlled emotion in the brown man's voice.

"My own people, sir," Johnson said.

Bernie nodded his head. He said, "You don't want to take Mao with you, I take it? Mrs. Carter doesn't want him, Captain Stein tells me."

"I'm fond of Mao," Johnson said. "But it would be difficult, sir. Regulations. He might have to go into quarantine, I understand. Anyway, I've just been somebody who feeds him, you see. He's always been—well, Mr. Carter's cat."

"They're that way sometimes," Nora said. "Aren't you, Mao?"

Mao twitched the tip of his long tail. He said, "Ow-uh," his voice as soft, as murmurous, as Nora's. He resumed purring.

"It's too bad," Bernie said. "Perhaps they'll find somebody to adopt him. Otherwise—well, they'll have to kill him, of course. They'll call it 'putting him to sleep.' Just as, when somebody dies, we prefer to say they've 'passed away.' What they do nowadays, I understand, is to put them in an airtight box and pump out the—"

"All right, Bernie," Nora said. "All *right*."

Her voice went up a little. Mao turned his head and looked at her over his shoulders. He looked at her upside down.

"I'm sorry, Mao," Nora told the cat. "I didn't mean to scare you."

But Mao gave no sign of being scared. He moved a little, snuggling more firmly in his newfound lap.

"I'll get his carrying box," Johnson said. "You'll have to hold him pretty tight, Miss Curran. He hates the box. He thinks it means the veterinarian."

Mao's voice wasn't soft at all after he heard the snap of the carrying box's catch as Johnson opened it. His long lithe body was all enraged muscle when Nora put him into the box, and Bernie closed the lid on him, with Johnson standing guard against escape. He screamed indignation all the way down to the Fifty-seventh Street ramp.

"Whatever made you think I wanted a cat?" Nora said, when they went down the ramp. At the sound of her voice, Mao said, "Wow-oh-wowouwau," at the top of his voice, which had a very high top. "It's all right, Mao," Nora said. "We're almost home."

"The way you talked about this cat you used to have," Bernie said. "The cat you called Diogenes. The way your voice sounded. I know the sounds of your voice, dear."

Bernie carried Mao in his box into the elevator— Mao and his toilet pan and a bag of something rather revoltingly called Klean Kitty. Nora carried, in a smaller bag, several jars of a ground beef meant for human infants. Mao yelled all the way up to the fifth floor. In the apartment, he quit talking. There was too much to smell. When he went into the bedroom, Nora said, "All right this time. But don't think you're going to sleep with me."

Bernie laughed, softly.

"I don't see what's funny," Nora said. She looked up at the tall man with such red hair. "Oh, all right," Nora Curran said.

"I'll claim visiting privileges," Bernie told her.

They found a place in the small kitchen for Mao's toilet pan, and poured Klean Kitty into it. "He'll probably scratch it all over the kitchen," Nora said. "The things you get me into, Bernie." She put down a bowl of water. She got an aluminum piepan out of a cupboard and put a teaspoonful of junior beef into it.

Mao came out to inspect the arrangements. He did not seem to disapprove.

He did speak loudly when they closed him out of the bedroom but that, Bernie told him, was something he would have to get used to.

* * * * *

Philip Whitmore called at a quarter of seven to say

he'd be a little late; that he had got tied up. He thought he could make it by seven-thirty and was she all right? Janet said she was fine, and there was an undercurrent of laughter in her voice to prove it. She also said that she had steaks under running cold water to thaw them. "I thought maybe—" Phil said, but she said, "Steaks. Here," and was firm about it.

She was wearing "at home" trousers—a yellow print, flecked with green, and a sleeveless blouse which picked up the yellow. The soft printed material flowed about her legs as she moved. He liked many things in yellow, including walls. But not, for reasons he had never been able to explain, bed linens. He had not mentioned that the first time they had been in bed together. Neither of them had mentioned anything that long-ago Sunday evening when, after two cocktails in front of a bouncing fire, they had decided dinner could wait. It was much later on that he admitted he had a thing against colored sheets. Colored pillow cases, too. Even when the color was yellow.

So—

It was seven-thirty-five when the buzzer rasped.

She stood on the landing and watched him climb the stairs, one shoulder just perceptibly lower than the other. How could I have been such a fool as not to know, to let doubt and uncertainty tangle in my mind? He was carrying what was clearly a bottle in a brown paper bag. He was fond of champagne. She had never told him she could take champagne or leave it alone. It had never been that important.

He put the champagne—Tattinger brut—in the refrigerator before he took her in his arms. He held her off a little and looked at her. Then he said, "Good." She said, "Very good, Philip dear." Then he made martinis to start with. Champagne would, as always, be for later.

"Had to do the piece over, of course. All set up and we had to scrap it. Piece about his war with the news media apparently being over. Or perhaps just in an armistice. The appointment of a known liberal to the FCC. Giving friends of the broadcasting industry an almost sure majority. Wow! So I flew down to Washington to look for leaks. How do they feel at your shop, Jan?"

"Apprehensive. That now it will probably be this man Whiteside. Who hates all IBC stands for. All Clay stood for. Oh—and Ronald Latham has been reassigned. Five-minute bit at noon on Saturdays. Keeping our chins up, I guess you'd call it."

"I doubt it will be Whiteside," Phil said. "They doubt it in Washington. A little too—well, too obvious even for them. A neutral, probably. Somebody nobody's ever heard of. Line I'm taking, anyway. Along with the polite assumption that the President didn't know about Streeter's—well, conflict of interest is one way of putting it. Selling out is another. Of course, we on the *Chronicle* never prejudge anybody."

"Not to be caught at it, anyway."

"Dear child, we are impartial in our reporting of the news. Opinion is expressed only in the editorial columns. And our commentators express only their own views. This impartiality is shared by all the country's leading newspapers. Including the Chicago *Tribune*."

There was only one thing to say to that. Janet said, "Yeah?"

Phil went out to see if the steaks were thawed. They were. He made a second round of martinis. They sipped. He turned and looked at her. He looks at me so hard, sometimes, Janet thought. He said, "Your eyes look—oh, as if you weren't thinking about this damn Streeter business at all. As if you were thinking about something else entirely. Would you rather talk about something else, dear?"

"Well," Janet Osborne said. "On a different subject—there were yellow sheets on the bed, Phil. When I changed the bed this morning, I put on white sheets."

They finished their drinks rather more rapidly than they usually did. Than they had for a long time.